Whirlwind of Desire

Laws of Passion, Volume 2

Amara Holt

Published by Amara Holt, 2024.

Copyright © 2024 by Amara Holt

All rights reserved.

No part of this book may be reproduced, distributed, or transmitted in any form or by any means, including photocopying, recording, or other electronic or mechanical methods, without the prior written permission of the author, except in the case of brief quotations in book reviews.

This is a work of fiction. Names, characters, places, and incidents are the product of the author's imagination or are used fictitiously. Any resemblance to actual events, organizations, locales, or persons, living or dead is coincidental and is not intended by the authors.

PROLOGUE

Zoey

16 YEARS OLD

I brushed my forehead and shifted my attention back to the canvas in front of me. I bit the tip of my lip, indecisive about the color shade I would use.

Through the partially open door of my room, I heard my brother coming home. Whenever Malcolm was in our town, he always invited the state governor over for dinner with us. They were inseparable.

It had been eight years since Malcolm moved to Springfield to take over all of Grandpa's businesses, dedicating himself completely to our country's politics. The pride of my father and his grandfather.

I wished I had a fraction of Malcolm's seriousness, but we were opposites in every way. Perhaps it was because he had inherited most of his genes from his mother's side of the family.

I got up from my stool and grabbed a damp cloth, wiping away the paint smudges.

I slowly pushed open the door, tiptoeing and tilting my head slightly over the railing on the second floor, listening to the voices of the two men.

I could even recognize the way he breathed in a room full of people and completely without light.

From up here, his golden hair, slicked to the side, and the impeccable suit covering his body. Always like that, methodical, never expecting anything different from him, his movements like a lion ready to pounce, never looking at anyone for too long. Calculating, I had never seen him say a word out of place, meticulous, paying attention to everything.

That might easily classify me as a stalker...

But it was just me, being a true obsessive about my brother's best friend.

I walked slowly towards the stairs but only descended the first few steps, watching the two men, both tall, as my brother seemed to be talking about one of his projects.

Malcolm caught me red-handed, raising an eyebrow when he saw me standing there.

"Zozo, do you want something?" The way he called me made me sound like a ten-year-old. How could William see me as a woman when Malcolm always treated me like a baby?

"Oh..." I cleared my throat when William turned his casual gaze towards me.

He had never looked at me the way he looked at those other women he dated, always with disinterested glances. After all, I was just his best friend's little sister.

"You know I don't like being called that nickname anymore." A pout formed on my lips.

"To me, you will always be my little sister." He winked playfully.

William had already diverted his gaze from me; nothing caught his attention for long, and I was just something bland in front of him.

"Will you stay for dinner, William?" I asked, making all the emotion in my voice clear. The governor turned his gaze back to me.

"Yes," he replied out of politeness, and because I was his friend's sister.

William would never see me as the woman I was becoming; he thought I would always be a child.

"Are you bothering them again, dear?" I felt Mom's arm around my shoulder.

I looked a lot like her; we were both short, with long black hair that matched our slightly tanned skin.

"You know our Zozo never bothers us, right, Claire?" My brother said affectionately to my mom.

Malcolm was from my father's first marriage. My father's love story began sadly when he lost his first wife to postpartum depression, where Violet ended up taking her own life, leaving Dad with a newborn son. My father loved his wife deeply and became a disillusioned man when it came to love. He didn't even believe he could love again. It took many years before my father and Mom started a relationship.

My brother always said that Mom was the missing key in Dad's life, and that I was their salvation, which made me extremely protected by both a father and a brother. Malcolm didn't know the word limit when it came to obsessively controlling everything around him.

"I just came to ask if William was staying for dinner, Mom," I declared, flashing one of my sly smiles.

"Oh, it will be an honor to have him here with us tonight, dear." Mom turned her gaze to William, who merely nodded at her.

"We'll have dinner and then go out, Claire," Malcolm didn't need to say where they were going; we all already knew.

The powerful men's club in California. A private place where only men were allowed, and women could only enter if accompanied.

And as if that wasn't enough, inside that club, there was everything—half-naked women dancing, lots of alcohol, nicotine... hatred... hatred... hatred...

Why could only men go out like this?

"It's all right, dear." Mom broke into my thoughts. "Have you finished the painting you said you would complete today, my daughter?"

"Not yet," I muttered, clearly showing my jealousy at that moment.

"Little sister," Malcolm caught my attention. "I'm glad you're infatuated with a man you can never have; it will ensure that no other man your age takes advantage of your situation."

At that moment, all I wanted was to tell Malcolm to screw off. What was wrong with liking an older man? It's not like I was his daughter or even from the same family.

Nothing, we had no relation. What were the chances of William ever looking at me as the woman I was becoming? *Zero*!

All I ever got were some pitying glances now and then.

But I didn't give up easily. I had spent years infatuated with that man; I wasn't going to give up now, just as I was nearing adulthood.

"Little brother, know that your words will never make me give up." My victorious smile made William narrow his eyes at me, as he always did when he wanted to scold me but couldn't speak up out of respect for my brother.

I turned my back on them, able to hear their conversation:

"If I ever find out you looked at my sister with interest, I'll cut off what you call a dick!" They thought I wasn't listening, but I was.

"Don't worry, she'll always be the annoying girl who keeps declaring her feelings for me." I could have sworn he was curling his lip as he always did.

All of that should have made me give up on William Fitzgerald, but on the contrary, I wanted him even more, and I wouldn't stop until I had him.

CHAPTER ONE

Zoey

Three years later...

I raised my arms while dancing to *"Red" by Taylor Swift*. I loved dancing, forgetting everything around me, *just dancing...*

"DAUGHTER!" My mother's loud shout made me turn my face to see her looking like she had called me a million times.

With a somewhat forced smile, I grabbed the remote from my bed and turned down the volume.

"Yes, Mom?" I asked with my best innocent performance, knowing she and Dad hated loud music.

"Scarlett is here; with that loud music, she can't hear anything," Mom concluded with a grumble.

"But Scarlett can come in," I replied, as my friend was practically like family.

"It seems she's in a hurry; if she comes in, you know you'll just delay her." Mom knew how I would dawdle when getting ready.

"She didn't even text me." I frowned in confusion.

"Have you considered it might be urgent?" Turning her back, Mom made a move to leave. "And don't forget to take your cell phone if you go out, dear."

"Yes, after that day, forgetting again would be really dumb of me." I remembered the last time I forgot my phone and almost ended up at the police station until I proved I had actually left it with all my cards inside, allowing me to make a call.

"*Zozo*, that's the kind of thing you always say and end up forgetting again." Mom looked back over her shoulder.

"You're right." I rolled my eyes, knowing how forgetful I was. "I'll just change clothes and head out, Mom."

She nodded and left the room. Scarlett not having entered my house meant it was really urgent, plus she would soon head back to campus. Since we graduated high school, our time together had become more scarce.

Scar had moved to study at Harvard just like all the Fitzgeralds. It was as if having that surname automatically guaranteed a spot there. Now it was even easier because Christopher Fitzgerald, her cousin, was elected President of the United States, and her brother, Zachary Fitzgerald, was the Vice President.

It had always been Scar's dream to study at Harvard. Even knowing she would get into that college, she earned her place, being number *one* every year we studied together, the biggest *nerd* I had ever met.

I was proud of my friend, knowing I could never be a fraction of what she was. We were best friends for that reason, two opposites who met.

Unlike Scarlett, I'm more of a dreamer. Maybe my feet were always in the clouds, as my dad said.

I changed into a pair of high heels and a denim skirt, since I lacked height. A short shirt exposed a bit of my belly but not enough to reveal my small belly button jewel. According to Scar, that was the second biggest crazy thing I had ever done in my life; the first was having an unrequited crush on her cousin.

I grabbed my phone from the bed and left the room. Through the front window, I could see my friend standing by her convertible.

I didn't even take my car from the garage, heading straight outside, knowing we were probably going out. I descended the few steps from the porch.

"Get in." Scarlett leaned over, opening the door to her car.

"What's so urgent that you couldn't even come in?" I said, leaving my phone on my lap.

"Geez, what a delay." Scarlett put on her sunglasses and started the car.

"So, what do you want from me?" I turned my face to her, not understanding.

"It's the grand opening of one of Gucci's new stores, and of course, I was invited." She gave one of her smug smiles. "And you're coming with me..."

"*Geez*, did it not cross your mind that I might have other commitments and might not be able to go?"

"And do you?" Scar looked at me with mischief, knowing I would cancel anything to attend such an event.

"Of course not." I burst into a hearty laugh. "How did you get this invite?"

"Simple, I know one of the managers of the new store..."

"Are you seeing him?" I widened my eyes.

"No!" She had a scolding tone in her voice. "Although Olavo is cute, he's just a friend I met at college when he came to give a lecture."

"So he's older than you?"

"Yes." She drummed her fingers on the steering wheel as if it were nothing.

"Funny how me liking an older man is a big deal, but you with an older man isn't?" I retorted with a grimace.

"The thing is, I met this older man recently; you've known William since we were in kindergarten..."

"And he's never stopped being hot," I interrupted with a dreamy smile.

"That look of yours scares me," Scar whispered.

"All I wanted was one chance for him to see me as the woman I am, not that clumsy girl anymore... *well*... I'm still clumsy, *but... damn*, I'm a woman." I shrugged.

"He has too much respect for your brother to ever be interested in you," Scarlett said what I already knew.

Malcolm would apparently always be our major obstacle, or rather, my major obstacle.

"I thought you'd get over this crush when William got engaged to Keith..."

"That relationship is faker than my gel nails," I cut her off.

"How do you know?"

"Simple, your cousin is too cold to be in a real relationship, and if it were for love, he'd feel jealous. In this case, he doesn't; they live hours apart, it's all staged, fake to throw off the photographers." I shrugged, confident in my intelligence when it came to William.

"Geez, now you're really scaring me, friend." Scar chuckled.

"Where are we going?" I asked, since she hadn't revealed our destination.

"To the mall, we need clothes for the event." We exchanged a knowing smile, as we both loved shopping together.

CHAPTER TWO

William

As long as the nails slid across my chest, I closed my eyes, simply feeling that light friction.

"Can you take the blindfold off now, Governor?" The woman purred, sounding like a purring cat.

"I'll take it off and I want you to leave," I declared, getting up from the bed.

I shouldn't have come home so late and spent almost the entire morning in bed. There were few women who could keep up with me, and when I found one, I used and abused it.

I focused my attention on the redhead sprawled on my bed. Her hands were cuffed, but the cuffs weren't too tight, so she managed to slide her nails across my chest, her legs secured in a strap keeping them bent to the side and completely exposed to me.

Veronica, that was her name; if there was one thing I never forgot, it was the names of the women who slept with me, all to avoid the risk of repeating myself. Consecutive sex opened up a chance for personal talks, so I didn't repeat.

I grabbed my robe from beside the bed, made of a thin fabric, used just to cover my body when I was too lazy to go to my closet. I tied it around my waist and leaned over the girl.

First, I removed the strap from her long legs, watching her stretch them, then I unlocked the cuffs, freeing her. Lastly, the blindfold, revealing the green eyes of the redhead. A lazy smile spread across her lips.

"I'm surprised it's already morning or rather..." Her eyes wandering over my covered body and then focusing on my face. "I'm not surprised."

She sat up on the bed, getting on her knees, wanting to hold onto my shoulder, but with a step back, I moved away from her.

"You need to go, Veronica, I have matters to attend to," my tone left no room for a second round of sex, my body was satisfied, completely cooled off for another round.

"Are you sure, Governor..." She raised her hand, touching her pointed breasts, my weakness, I focused on those pink nipples and clenched my fists.

"I'm sure," I continued firmly, my dick didn't even show any sign of wanting another round of sex.

The redhead shrugged and crawled to the side of the bed, getting up. She was a tall woman, the type of model who never missed my bed.

The doorbell rang in my apartment. Only a few people had the freedom to come up to my floor, so I could already guess who it was. I just hoped it wasn't my assistant giving one of his speeches early in the morning.

"Baby, there's a car waiting for you at the back of the building," I told the girl before turning towards the door.

"Will you call me, Governor?" They all asked this question after sex.

"Yes," the answer was always the same, but obviously a lie; I never called again, and the number they had was my assistant's, never mine.

Justin knew everything about my life; he was the one who made them sign a confidentiality contract before we slept together. In fact, he sent it online and I just asked for the signature. I couldn't risk having my name tainted on some site as a traitor.

I headed to the elevator without caring about the woman there getting dressed, pressed the button to open it, but when it opened, I was faced with Keith, my fiancée, who walked in immediately.

"What took you so long?" She grumbled while looking around. The door to my room was open, where she could see the woman. "Wow... I'm jealous now."

"Hello, fiancée," I mocked, putting my hand in the pocket of my robe.

"I'm wondering where you find one of these; can we share?" Keith's eyes sparkled as she glanced at me.

"All yours." I shrugged, watching Veronica now fully dressed enter the room, the tall woman met my gaze.

"I hope to see you soon, Governor," she whispered shyly, and they thought I believed that soft talk.

"Or we could meet." Keith drew Veronica's attention, who looked at her. "Nice to meet you, Keith Moore..."

The two were tall and exchanged a quick hug.

"Oh, I know her." It was impossible not to know Keith; she was the gateway for any woman wanting to enter the fashion world with the best contacts.

Keith was a well-known model, the most famous socialite of that generation. And like me, she kept a good part of her private life hidden from the news.

"Here's my number, call me." My fiancée handed her card to her.

At that moment, I stopped being the center of attention for Veronica. She was obviously fascinated by Keith. At least she got something out of sleeping with me.

Holding the card, Veronica left my apartment, and I was left alone with my fiancée.

"I didn't know you were in town." I furrowed my brow and headed to the kitchen, knowing she would follow me.

"I just arrived. I need my fiancé today," she said, drawing my attention while I was preparing the coffee maker.

"You need, do you?"

"Yes, I have a very important event, and who better than my fiancé to accompany me?" Keith leaned over the kitchen island. "Since you offered, I'll take a cup of coffee..."

"Hold on, impatient, I haven't gotten to that part yet." I smiled, rolling my eyes.

"You will, won't you, William?"

"I need to check my schedule with Justin," I said as the doorbell rang again. "By the way, it must be him; he always comes by to see if everything is alright when I take too long to reply to his messages."

I mocked, leaving the coffee maker to brew, and went to the elevator, opening it to find my assistant there.

"From your outfit, I understand why you didn't reply to me," he immediately grumbled, entering my apartment. "Hello, Keith, dear..."

"Hi, Justin," Keith greeted him. The two got along very well; after all, Keith's influence helped me maintain my image as a romantic man.

"It's good to see you in town; I was thinking about you. After all, you two need to appear together more often; you're getting too distant, and people are starting to notice." Justin grabbed the cups from the holder, placing them on the counter.

"The perfect occasion has arisen today. Come with me to the Gucci collection launch event; I'm sponsoring them, and I need my fiancé's company." She flashed a big smile while I bit my lip.

I hated those kinds of events; too much pretense and too many of those people around us. Nothing new in the world I lived in.

"Perfect, perfect, perfect." Justin clapped his hands at what Keith said.

"Looks like we have an event tonight." I filled the cups with steaming coffee, paying attention to their enthusiasm about the brand.

CHAPTER THREE

Zoey

"How do I look?" I asked, turning around to face Scarlett.
"You're asking that? — My friend rolled her eyes. — Beautiful as always, and me?"

Scar was wearing a long dress that shimmered softly as she moved. Its neckline was modest, not revealing much.

"Ready to catch the boss?" I gave a mischievous smile.

"I've told you, he's just a friend..."

"A friend you want to catch." I turned back around and gave myself one last look in the mirror, making sure I looked stunning.

My dress was navy blue, hugging my curves nicely, with a side cut that revealed my leg when I walked. The high heels on my feet were a must. My makeup was subtle, just to highlight my black eyes.

Since we were at the mall, we took the opportunity to have our hair done at a salon, getting it ready.

"Your brother giving you this apartment made me realize I want to live on my own," I said, leaving Scarlett's room.

"Now that Zachary and Sav are living in Washington D.C., this apartment would be vacant. Zach said this place is part of his past. Whether it was or wasn't, it's going to be my future now." Scarlett shrugged. "Even though I spend little time here in Sacramento."

"Now that I'm officially working at mom's gallery, I'll see if I can rent an apartment..."

"Don't your parents have apartments?"

"They do, but I want something to be able to say that I got it with my own paintings." I grabbed my clutch, which contained my phone.

"I understand what you mean," Scarlett agreed as we left the apartment.

My parents owned an art gallery, where mom was the lead artist, with some of her friends participating as house artists. My dad managed everything with a team of employees. They also had several businesses throughout California.

My dream was always to work with them, to have an exhibition of my own paintings. Since I was a child, I would sit next to mom, perfecting my craft. If there was one thing I loved, it was getting lost in the paints, not caring about getting messy.

We opted to take a rideshare, since we weren't sure if we would be drinking alcohol.

I sat in the back seat next to Scarlett, and behind our car, there was a black car.

"Girl, you still pretend to be a normal person with your security right behind?" I mocked her softly.

"Zachary and dad have absurd protection for all the members of our family," she grumbled, rolling her eyes.

"Luckily, I'm not as influential as you." I shrugged.

"But you'd be crazy for a Fitzgerald, I'd run from one of them just because of all these shadows," my friend had a note of discontent in her voice. "Privacy, I don't even know what that is."

"I'd be happy with just one night with William, I wonder how he must be in bed," I murmured, opening a wicked smile.

"We know you'd never be satisfied with just one night," Scarlett retorted, teasing me "and trust me, if there's one thing I don't think about, it's my cousin's performance."

With a faint chuckle, we shifted the focus of our conversation. We came up with thousands of theories about who would be at the event.

It wasn't long before the car stopped in front of the event. Our door was opened by a man from the outside, with Scar stepping out first, followed by me. There were many flashes directed at us, which was typical for such a place.

With a smile on my face, I walked on, the focus being mainly on Scarlett. After all, she was a Fitzgerald, the cousin of the President of the United States, the sister of the Vice President, and also the cousin of the Governor of California. Well, I was a Beaumont, but the success of our surname was all Malcolm's and his discreet life as the Governor of Illinois.

We announced our names at the entrance and were let in. My arm intertwined with Scar's. I looked around, admiring everything. I loved that kind of place; in fact, I enjoyed being in the spotlight.

"Do you smell that?" I whispered to Scar with a bit of mischief.

"The smell of real leather, luxury brand." We exchanged glances.

"You got it." Next to us, a waiter passed by with a tray of champagne glasses.

I took one in my hand and gently brought it to my lips. There were many clothing pieces on display, and we soon headed towards the door where the runway would be.

"Scarlett?" The deep voice, the same voice that was a melody to my ears, spoke behind us.

Scar was the first to turn around, followed by me, knowing exactly who we would see there.

"Cousin." Scarlett smiled at her cousin.

"I didn't know you'd be here, shouldn't you be at college?" he asked, furrowing his brow, treating my friend as if she were a little girl.

"I'm not, as you can clearly see." Scarlett shrugged.

Standing next to William was his fiancée. The two made a beautiful couple, which made me even more annoyed. They were tall, matched perfectly, even in their clothes. The fact that Keith was incredibly beautiful and nice only made it harder to hate her for being with the man I wanted.

"Well, I hope you know what you're doing." William didn't even look in my direction, not even a glance.

"Yes, Will, I know exactly what I'm doing," Scarlett always confronted all the Fitzgeralds, and being the only female cousin, they were all protective of her. "Let's go, Zozo, it was a pleasure to see you, Keith..."

My friend pulled me along, using the nickname I hated, especially when said in front of William.

"I feel the same, dear," Keith declared with her melodious and calm voice.

"I'll be keeping an eye on you two," William made it clear that any plan Scarlett had to go out with another man was out the window.

I knew the *"I'll be keeping an eye on you two"* was out of respect for my brother. He obviously wouldn't be keeping an eye on me with any ulterior motives.

We moved away from them, my friend's steps were so heavy that her huffing was audible.

"Damn, I didn't know he'd be here. William just ruined all my plans," she grumbled. "If I go out with Olavo now, I'll give him a reason to tell my brother, and then I'll get one of those lectures from them..."

"And in the end, I was right," I teased, giving her a nudge.

"I wanted to come to this event, I love this brand and Olavo would just be a distraction, but as you can see, your beloved interrupted me." We approached the seats.

"I think it's time for you to reveal you're no longer a virgin," I teased.

"Oh God! I'm never doing that, let them think I'm the family's little girl. After all, you didn't even tell..."

"My mom knows..."

"Mine too, and that's quite enough. — We both shared a knowing smile.

Our lives were very similar, but hers was even more private than mine.

CHAPTER FOUR

Zoey

Scarlett remained silent throughout the entire show. I never thought I'd say this, but William's presence in a place wasn't exactly welcome at that moment. He ruined all my expectations for the night.

After all, just because I envisioned my future with him didn't mean I was going to stay pure and untouched for him. He went around sleeping with any woman. Why did I need to be untouched?

After announcing her engagement to Keith, the rumors stopped, but knowing William as I did, I was almost certain he must make women sign some confidentiality agreement. The governor could deceive an entire country with that engagement, but he didn't fool me.

They didn't look at each other with love; it was as if it were something robotic.

Fortunately, or unfortunately, William and Keith sat in front of Scarlett and me. This made our dissatisfaction even more evident.

"Can we go to a club later, and you invite your friend?" I whispered close to Scar's ear, making sure no one else heard.

My friend looked at me, her eyes starting to sparkle at that moment.

"Great." She winked.

Apparently, not everything was lost at that moment. The show was coming to an end when Keith was invited to walk the runway. Elegantly, she did, receiving applause from everyone. William's fiancée gave a brief speech about the partnership she had with Gucci.

It was undeniable. Keith was amazing, not at all like most snobbish models. William could have found a fiancée easy to hate, which definitely wasn't the case.

Finishing her speech, Keith returned to sit next to William, and the lights in the room were turned on, allowing guests to mingle. Ambient music began to play. I stood up from my chair along with Scarlett.

As I turned my face, I spotted two men approaching.

"Head towards them," my friend whispered in my ear, making both of us start walking away from William.

We approached the two men, and I assumed one of them must be Olavo.

"I'm glad you could make it," one of them said, coming closer to Scar and giving her a kiss on the cheek.

"Are you kidding? I wouldn't miss this event for anything." Scarlett was passionate about all those brands.

"This is your friend Zoey?" he asked, directing a look at me.

"Yes, Zoey, this is Olavo." We exchanged a quick look, and I focused on the man in front of me.

"Nice to meet you." I gave him a kiss on the cheek.

Olavo introduced his friend Mike, who was only slightly taller than me, nothing compared to my governor, who was tall and had a scowling look.

"My cousin is here." Scarlett rolled her eyes as she spoke. "Not that it's a problem for you, it's more of a problem for me. Everyone treats me like I'm still a child."

"It's all right, there's a bar nearby, we can go there in a few minutes, I just need to talk to a few more clients." Winking, Olavo moved away with his friend.

I was left alone with Scarlett, making a face at her.

"Look, I'll stay with you out of courtesy, but I'm not going out with that guy." I pouted.

"He's not your type, huh?" My friend forced a smile.

"Not at all, he's short compared to the tall men I usually date." I set a standard for tall men, all to practice in my dreams with the governor.

"Sorry, friend," she whispered.

"Friends are *for* this, right, even though Olavo isn't attractive either." I continued pouting.

"Yeah, he's not very good-looking, but he's nice. I'm testing a new type of man." She shrugged.

"In your vast experience with men." I struggled not to laugh.

"Okay, okay... I'm not looking for anything serious, maybe just a hookup. Olavo is the kind of guy who doesn't brag, doesn't tell everyone he's been with, so..." she bit the corner of her lip.

I lifted my gaze, seeing her cousin approaching.

"Here comes our delicious torment for the night," I whispered, noticing that William was alone.

Scarlett made me smile when she twisted with discomfort upon realizing her cousin was approaching, and she turned to stand beside me when she noticed he would stop in front of us.

"Who were you talking to?" The question was directed at Scarlett, after all, she was his family.

"A friend." She shrugged.

"How do you know him?"

"I know him," I spoke up to cover for her. "Olavo had coffee with me at my favorite café, and since then we've been chatting."

Even if William told my brother, it would be easy to clear my name because there were only two men concerned about me, unlike Scarlett who had many.

"Does your brother know?" I think that was the first time he focused his gaze on me.

"It's not like I'm still ten years old; I'm nineteen and I take care of myself just fine." I didn't divert my eyes from his, those clear blue eyes.

"Family girls shouldn't be going out with men." I rolled my eyes, making a face.

"Women, *we're women*" I corrected him, emphasizing *women*. "Being part of a family doesn't make us any different from all the other women you've been with. You should worry about your fiancée, Governor. She will be your future wife, not the two of us!"

I raised my nose with a smug pout forming on my lips. Did I, for the first time, leave the governor speechless?

"I hope you both know what you're getting into." His gaze shot daggers at me. For the first time, I received that stare for longer than usual.

William even dared to let his gaze linger on my cleavage. He might have thought it wasn't a big deal, but the way he looked and quickly averted his eyes was as if he were mentally cursing himself.

Turning his back, the governor left, leaving me alone with Scarlett.

"Friend!" She immediately turned, grabbing my hands to keep from freaking out. "What was that? You confronted William, is the world ending and I didn't know about it?"

"Come on, he called us girls. I'm no longer a girl; I'm a woman, we're women," I said firmly.

"And believe me, he devoured you with his eyes. I saw how he checked out your breasts. *Friend, friend, friend...* Do you think we have your long-awaited breakthrough?"

"From that man, I expect nothing more," I muttered, shrugging.

William had shown so many times that he wanted nothing to do with me that this was just another instance among many.

CHAPTER FIVE

Zoey

I was questioning how strange my friend's taste in men was. The conversation with Oliver was so boring that I was even starting to feel sleepy. Meanwhile, Scarlett continued animatedly chatting with him.

The good thing was that Oliver's friend noticed I wasn't interested and moved on to another territory. I stayed in that boring bar for as long as Scar wanted. The other man found a woman and ended up leaving earlier. That promised me a nice night of sleep, *alone*.

Once alone again, I concluded that men just weren't the same as they used to be, and it was probably due to my extremely high standards for the male gender.

There was a time when I thought about staying a virgin for my governor, but that idea faded when I saw him kissing a woman at a party my brother was hosting at his house. I had just turned eighteen, had my driver's license, but wasn't invited to that party. Nonetheless, I sneaked in and sneaked out the same way.

I was deluded to think that William wasn't sleeping around with any model who crossed his path.

I think that was the most exciting scene I had ever seen up close. His strong hands roaming the body of that woman, holding her leg, sliding his finger between her legs, without even stopping the kiss.

It was too much. I concluded that I would never be experienced to that extent, and I set my mind on losing my virginity. I lost it, and it was horrible. Not pleasant at all. The second time was with another man; it was a bit better than the first, but not wonderful. The third time felt like going back to the first, horrible.

I allowed myself a fourth time, and that was good, not incredibly good, but just good, would be the perfect rating.

"Friend?" Scarlett touched my shoulder as if she had been calling me for some time and I hadn't heard. "Shall we go?"

"Let's go," I affirmed, almost jumping off the stool.

"You're bored, aren't you?" Scar twisted her lip.

"Not anymore," I mocked.

We headed out of the bar. The night was a bit chilly, and I rubbed my arms, regretting not bringing a coat.

"Oliver is driving, do you want us to drop you off at home first?" Scarlett asked.

"Oh, no need. I'll call a car here." I took my phone out of my handbag.

"Are you sure?"

"Friend, go enjoy your nerdy guy," I went back to mocking her; Oliver was so dull he didn't even drink alcohol.

I practically pushed my friend to go enjoy her guy. I stood there alone watching Scarlett leave with Oliver, while her bodyguards followed, and obviously, her parents, brother, cousins, and uncles would know she was with a man. But that wasn't something we needed to worry about at that moment.

I opened my app, entered my destination, and then, with a start, I was shocked to see a black SUV pull up in front of me.

At that moment, I thought about running, but that car was accompanied by two more of the same style. The window rolled down, and I heard that deep voice I knew so well.

"Get in," was all he said. His face wasn't visible, but I knew it was the governor.

It was just a matter of grabbing the handle and getting in. *But..., but...* my rebellious side didn't want to give in to the governor at that moment. The fact that he called me a girl still made me furious.

Despite everything I did to flaunt that I had become a woman, and he continued to call me *girl*?

"I don't need a ride, I've already called a car," I said without looking toward the window.

I looked around, pretending to search for the car I hadn't even called yet. *I was good at throwing tantrums.*

"I'm not repeating myself. Get in the damn car, now!" he didn't ask, he commanded.

His commanding tone made my whole body shiver, even that small spot between my legs.

"You don't boss me around. I already said my car is almost here." I planted my feet on the ground, at that moment not wanting to see William's handsome face.

In a jolt backward, my eyes widened when the door on the other side opened, and through it, I saw the tall man step out. Handsome, impeccable, and angry.

William came towards me, his eyes glaring at mine.

"Get in the damn car, now!" he growled in a low tone, looking around as if to make sure we weren't being watched.

"Make me. You don't control me." I pouted, raising my face.

"Zoey, don't make me pick you up and put you in this car," he roared in a primal manner.

"We both know you wouldn't do that. We're in public..." I didn't have time to finish my sentence when his large hands quickly grabbed my leg from behind, lifting me onto his lap and swiftly placing me in the car seat.

"*Damn stubborn girl*" he muttered, slamming the door.

In less than a minute, William was sitting beside me, whispering something I didn't even understand.

"What's your problem, *huh*?" he asked, turning his face towards me and, before I could respond, spoke to his driver. "Let's stop by the Beaumont residence and drop Zoey off there."

"My problem? I don't have any problem. You're just wasting your precious time with me. You could be at your apartment with your fiancée, but here you are, alone. Could it be because this engagement is fake?" I said all at once, without filter, unloading all my theories.

"You must be crazy!" He ran his hand through his hair, agitated.

"I know you well, Governor. I know that this engagement is not real and never has been. Only a fool would believe it," I continued with my mockery.

"On what basis are you saying that?" He squinted his eyes, and at that moment, I thought he might actually grab me by the neck.

"I just know." I shrugged my shoulders.

I wasn't going to reveal how I knew. He'd think I was literally crazy for knowing so many details about him.

CHAPTER SIX

Zoey

Great, now I was in the governor's car, being driven home as if I were a teenager.

"Why were you alone? Where is my cousin?" Damn, he changed the subject, and it was an even worse one.

"She went with another car," I muttered, keeping my attention on the window, refusing to look at William, because I knew if I did, all my walls might crumble in the face of how much I desired that man.

"I thought you did everything together. If she went in another car, and you... unless..."

"Wow, congratulations, Governor. You're learning a bit more about women." I rolled my eyes, being sarcastic.

"We're not talking about women, but two teenagers." At that moment, I turned my face abruptly.

"Teenagers? Are you serious? At nineteen, you still consider yourself a teenager?" My eyes met his; in the dim light of the car, the color of his eyes wasn't clear.

"From the family..."

"*Blah... blah... blah...*" I cut him off before he could start with that family story. "Don't think that just because we come from influential families, we want to marry pure and innocent. We're women like any other."

"What are you trying to say?" Even in the darkness of the car, the governor's face was marked with astonishment.

"Take it however you want." I turned my gaze back to the street, swearing I heard him growling like a caveman. Was all this because Scarlett was apparently with another man, even though I neither denied nor confirmed anything?

"You think you're very clever, don't you, Miss Beaumont?" That was the first time he addressed me that way.

Since Malcolm was his best friend, we'd developed a certain intimacy that allowed us to use first names.

"Was that a question?" I turned my gaze back to his.

William took his phone out of his suit, the screen lit up with a woman's name flashing.

"Strange, isn't it, a woman calling you, Governor?" I said with irony.

"It's none of your business," he retorted.

"If it were my fiancé, I wouldn't allow any woman to call him. What a liberal fiancée you have." I gave a small, provocative smile.

"That's probably why you don't even have a boyfriend..."

"The last one I was with even wanted to get engaged, but I don't usually get engaged with the first guy who comes along." I shrugged, watching him turn off his phone and put it back in his pocket.

"Does your family know about this?"

"Know what, exactly?" I was a master at provocation.

"That you're seeing other men?"

"I can take care of myself." William was starting to get more and more irritated with my vague responses.

"Not all men will want what's best for you..."

"Who says I want what's best for them? Being a wild girl suits me better." I bit the corner of my lip.

"Are you flirting with me, Miss Beaumont?"

"Far from it. You're my past. I've just grown up enough to realize that fairy tales don't exist and that being a good girl doesn't always work out. — At that moment, I wanted to sit on his lap and see what it would be like to run my hand over the governor's defined abdomen, the same abdomen I'd spent hours staring at on a website that photographed William during his morning run.

"To me, this smells more like wounded pride." William looked at me as if he wanted to decipher me.

"Don't think you're the best man when I've seen much better." I looked out the window casually.

I had nothing to lose. Anyway, the governor was never going to want anything with me, so I might as well play hard to get, making him think I no longer wanted anything to do with him.

"You're bluffing, I can smell your bluff from here," he declared, making me look into his eyes.

"And why would I bluff? Or did you really think I'd spend the rest of my life nursing an unrequited crush?" I needed to keep my chin up and my posture proud, otherwise, he would notice.

"Your eyes give you away. The way your pupils move, you're nervous, lying." He raised his hand when he saw me turn my face, his warm fingers brushing against my chin for the first time. "If you weren't the sister of my best friend, I'd teach you a lesson for being stubborn, I'd treat you like the woman you claim to be..."

His voice trailed off as I slightly parted my lips. A sigh escaped them as my whole plan went up in smoke, and he realized that I was still a completely deluded romantic.

"What would you do?" I asked daringly in a whisper.

"First, I would tie your wrists with my tie, then I'd drape your body over my lap. Being petite would make it easier for me to move you," he stopped speaking as the car began to slow down, *no, no, no...*

"What else?" I asked, but the tension had been broken.

The car stopped. William withdrew his fingers from my chin, and I wanted more of that touch. Why did he pull away? Damn that moment the car had to stop.

"Get out, Zoey," His voice no longer carried that same sensual tone, one I had never heard from him before; now it had taken on the tone of a governor, my brother's friend.

"Are you serious?" I widened my eyes, refusing to shrink away and leave with my tail between my legs.

"Get out of this damn car, now!" He growled as if trying to control himself.

"Don't ever touch me again, got it?" I fumbled around the seat looking for my small purse.

"Then stay away from me," he grunted, not taking his eyes off mine.

"If you tell my brother anything, or even about Scarlett, I'll tell everyone you tried to punish me." I flashed my best provocative smile, regaining my composure, showing that I hadn't been affected, even though deep down I could swear that if I twisted my underwear, it would drip from how wet I got just from the governor's fingers touching me.

"Are you blackmailing me?" He was clearly not expecting my reaction.

"Dear William, I know you understood what I meant." Grasping the car's door handle, I opened the door.

Long fingers gripped my wrist, and I turned my face before stepping out of the car.

"What I said can become reality if you think you can play with me." His face was close to mine, but I didn't act scared.

"Not everything in life is as the governor thinks it should be." I pulled my arm with a bit more force.

William grunted as I exited the car, my heels echoing on the sidewalk of my parents' house. From the warmth that spread through my body, I could swear he was in that car watching me. It was only when I entered the house that I heard the governor's car driving away.

CHAPTER SEVEN

Zoey

It was going to be one of those typical days when it's hard to get out of bed, especially with my phone constantly ringing beside me, the loud noise making me turn in bed, hitting the pillow beside me.

Without even checking the name on the screen, I answered the call, bringing the phone to my ear.

"*Hmm...*" I mumbled, still groggy.

"*Girl, are you still asleep?*" Scarlett's lively voice came through the line.

"Not everyone wakes up with your energy, unless you had a good fuck," I grumbled amidst my speech.

"*ZOEY!*" I pulled the phone slightly away from my ear at her shout.

"Damn, Scar" I retorted, opening my eyes to look at the white ceiling.

"*Aunt Abigail asked for help with organizing an event. She's having a meeting at her house with the women from the club, and asked if I wanted to come. I thought of you*" she was excited.

"That is if my mom hasn't already been invited." Rubbing my eyes, I said, knowing that my mom and Mrs. Abigail Fitzgerald were part of the same women's club.

"*Good point. I want to know if you're coming, girl. I'm heading back to campus tomorrow, and I want to spend a bit more time with my best friend...*"

"We could go somewhere other than that women's club." I pouted.

"*You know I can't say no to my family.*" I could swear she was making one of her pouty faces.

"And do you, by any chance, know how to say no to anyone?" I teased.

"*Are you coming or not?*" She ignored me.

"Of course, I'll go. I'll sacrifice myself to listen to those women talk about my man" I teased in a playful tone.

"*Speaking of which, no one at home has mentioned my night so far. I'm surprised, how did William stay silent?*" Scarlett declared, curious.

"Simple, yesterday he gave me a ride while I was waiting for my rideshare. He would have mentioned it, rest assured; those Fitzgeralds are very protective. But the game turned against him when he said he wanted to punish me..."

"*What?*" My friend clearly wanted to control herself from shouting.

"William likes aggressive sex? And I thought I knew everything about him. I know the governor doesn't look like the type who punches fluffy, but tying up? Spanking my ass? Oh, girl, I think I lived a dream." I ran my hand through my hair, imagining the scene.

"*Is that real? Like, really real? No delusion? Did William actually do that?*" Scarlett was as astonished as I was.

"I'm asking myself the same question. The proof it's real is that he hasn't said a word. — I flashed a small smile. — Scar, I don't know what got into that man to make him do that, well... maybe I provoked him."

I chuckled, starting to explain everything to her.

"PLEASE, MY DAUGHTER, don't get into any arguments with anyone about the governor," Mom asked as the car approached Mrs. Fitzgerald's house, William's mother.

"Those women think they have the right to say he's going to marry their little girl," I grumbled, rolling my eyes.

"I wonder if this obsessive thought of yours about the governor will ever pass." My mom sighed, glancing sideways at me.

"Mom, I just wanted a taste," I gave a brief, mocking smile.

"We both know it's not just that you want. You know your brother would never allow a relationship with William, even if the governor wanted you," my mom threw reality in my face.

"That's why William will never change his mind about me, all because of Malcolm. It's like they have this brotherhood that keeps the governor from looking at me." I shrugged my shoulders.

"Maybe your brother knows the type of friend he has and wants something much better for his sister," everything they told me seemed to go in one ear and out the other.

"I'd rather everyone think this crush of mine is just a passing phase," I teased, shrugging my shoulders.

"Sometimes I'm afraid of where this obsession of yours might lead," I didn't respond to my mom.

She was the only one who knew that everything I did wasn't just a crush, or maybe it could be. But growing up and becoming a teenager with the view of William as my prince charming made me more addicted to every movement of his life.

It could be just an addiction. After all, I didn't know about his personal life, how he acted at home, his struggles, his insecurities.

I would love to know, but we never had that level of intimacy. Whenever I tried to talk to him, it was like he had no patience to converse with a girl like me.

William always saw me as his best friend's little sister, even if I were to strip in front of him, he'd probably turn his back or even imagine me as my brother.

Determined should have been my last name because I wanted at all costs to have a taste of the governor, even if the barriers against me were enormous.

Pulling up in front of the Fitzgerald mansion, my mom's driver got out of his car and walked to my door, which I opened with Mom by my side.

The door to the house was soon opened, and as we approached, the housekeeper greeted me with a brief smile.

I believe I could even be considered a Fitzgerald by persistence.

"Hello, Margo." I returned the smile, approaching her, and without caring that she was just a housekeeper, I hugged her with a kiss on the cheek.

"Hello, dear. Mrs. Fitzgerald is waiting in the backyard with some guests who have already arrived."

I merely nodded as my mom grabbed my arm, as if trying to restrain my impulsive actions, because she already knew how I behaved around Abigail. But what could I do if William's mother even called me her dream daughter-in-law?

CHAPTER EIGHT

William

"Has Keith returned to New York?" my brother asked as my driver stopped the car in front of my parents' residence.

"Yes," I replied with a single word.

"You know, I really don't understand what your intention is with this engagement," Sawyer grumbled, wanting me to talk more about my relationship.

"Marriage? Isn't that the point of an engagement?" The doors were opened for me, and I grabbed my suitcase, watching my brother exit through the other door without waiting for it to be opened for him.

Sawyer let out a loud sigh. He was wearing light jeans with what looked like black boots, and a V-neck shirt. My brother was the opposite of all the Fitzgeralds. The only one who didn't want to go into politics, the only one who wanted tattoos, and even had a rock band, which he and his friends ended up disbanding due to a lack of time for rehearsals. Each member went their own way.

My brother was educated, a very good lawyer, he could be practicing his profession, passed all the tests, and was approved to practice. But apparently, nothing was good enough for him.

"Keith has nothing in common with you; even my shampoo has more chemistry than the two of them." I rolled my eyes.

"Since when have you noticed that?" I asked, seeing Margo open the door of the house as we approached.

"From the moment it could affect our family, making Mom feel guilty, it became my concern." Sawyer might be the black sheep of the family, but that didn't make him any less of a Fitzgerald.

"I'm going to marry Keith, and that won't reflect on anything." As I entered my parents' house, I could hear female voices. "What are those voices, Margo?"

My eyes met the housekeeper's.

"Mrs. Abigail is having a meeting with the women from the club." I curled my lip at what she said.

"I can't believe Mrs. Abigail invited us here for that meeting." Sawyer grumbled, about to turn and run.

"You both will be dragged there by force if you try to escape," obviously, Mom already knew our plans, which is why she omitted this little meeting.

"I'm the governor of California; I have much more to do." I retorted, turning around.

"You will!" My mom's reprimanding voice made me turn around again. "Both of you, and your cousin Christopher, won't be joining because a president has an entire country to take care of..."

"Seriously, Mom? Are you using hierarchical authority now?" I was debating whether to consider running away and then face the beast that was Mrs. Abigail or face another one of those foundation galas.

"Son, I need you. Auctioning off the governor would bring a lot of money to our organization." Mom supported underprivileged organizations in California, and those galas always raised a lot of money.

"Sawyer will go." I pushed my brother, who shot me an angry look.

"Yes, he will go too. Both of you will go. I bet if Zachary were here, he would agree without complaining." There was her emotional blackmail.

"We know he wouldn't." I rolled my eyes; we all hated that auction business.

"Son, please." Mom gave me that look she always used when she wanted to get something out of me.

I let out a long sigh, exchanged a look with my brother, knowing we wouldn't have an escape but would have to accept yet another mess.

"Fine, but I'm warning you now, just a one-hour dinner, no more," I set my conditions.

Sawyer, having no alternative, ended up agreeing as well.

"I'll take advantage of being here and go to Dad's office; he asked me to look at some of his documents." My brother passed by me.

"Are you finally going to take a case, my son?" Mom now had a hopeful look.

"We know Edward keeps giving me his legal cases to make me an official Fitzgerald lawman. But that's not what I'm going to do, just help him." Sawyer went up the stairs toward my father's office.

"Let him be, Mom; Sawyer will find his place." I winked.

"I wish he would at least work with Carter and Natalie, but he doesn't even want that." Mom shrugged her shoulders.

Carter and Natalie were my uncles, Christopher's parents, and were currently running their law firm in Washington DC, all to be closer to their only child, who was now the President of America.

"Don't pressure him; that will only make him more resentful. Sawyer needs to find his place in the world." I smiled at my mother, kissing the top of her head. "I'm going to the kitchen to get a glass of water and then I'll leave. If I'd known this was all you wanted my presence for, I wouldn't have come."

"If you hadn't come, you wouldn't have agreed to my request. I know my children." She smiled, turning and heading back to the rear of the house.

Alone, I went to the kitchen and got a glass, filling it from the filter, when I heard the sound of heels entering the room, but I didn't even bother to look. Until I heard that voice.

"You've fulfilled your part of the bargain," she had a soft tone; after Zoey had become a woman, her voice had changed, taking on a melodious and even gentle tone, but I never dared to mention that to her brother.

"With great effort, yes. But I might still change my mind." I turned around, holding the glass in my hand, while looking at the girl who, even in high heels, still seemed small.

Zoey was wearing a green dress with a few red flowers. The neckline was covered by an off-the-shoulder design with sleeves that fell below her shoulder; it was literally just an embellishment for the dress.

"You wouldn't do that; your loyalty to my brother would prevent you from doing so." On her slightly full lips, covered with some kind of lip gloss, appeared a smug smile.

I didn't respond, taking the glass to my mouth, drinking it all quickly, wanting to escape that conversation, or even Zoey's presence. After our last meeting, I began having thoughts about my best friend's sister that I should never have had.

I left the glass in the sink and turned toward the door where I had left my suitcase, wanting to leave my parents' house.

"William," the little thing called out to me again. I didn't turn around, but I could hear what she said. "My brother doesn't need to know about the punishment if you want to give it to me..."

I gripped the handle of the suitcase tightly, *damn it*! That girl seemed to live in a world where everything was fairy tales. Her always insolent manner sometimes drove me crazy.

Without responding, knowing that it was all my fault, even that dream where I spanked Zoey's ass until it turned red was my fault.

I needed a fuck, a fuck that wasn't my friend's sister.

CHAPTER NINE

Zoey

"Honey, that dress looks so beautiful on you," my mother said as soon as I came down the stairs of our house.

"Am I worthy of being swept away by a handsome man?" There was a hint of sarcasm in my voice. "After all, Malcolm won't be there today; he won't be the one paying for my dinner."

I rolled my eyes, knowing this would be my second year being auctioned off for dinner, and in the first year, my brother was the one who won me, all to keep me from going out with any other man.

"Even so, I didn't want my little girl up on that stage," Dad complained, adjusting his tie.

"Dad, it's for a good cause; it's a ball to raise funds. Even Scarlett will be at the auction." I gave one of my delicate smiles, hoping to make Dad understand that this wasn't an auction to sell his daughter's virginity.

"The Fitzgeralds have plenty of men in their family to make bids; I wouldn't be surprised if one of them ends up buying the dinner," my father said, echoing what we all had already suspected.

"I deeply hope you don't place a bid for mine," I grumbled, turning and heading toward the door.

I HADN'T SEEN THE GOVERNOR for days; I had the impression that he was ignoring me. Since our meeting at his parents' house, William had been spending more time locked away in the Capitol. It must have been just my impression, as I had never posed any threat to the governor.

I walked alongside my mother through the luxurious ballroom; everything was perfectly organized in the Abigail Fitzgerald style. She was always known for throwing the best social events.

I looked for Scarlett; I wanted to be by her side so we could catch up on things.

I found my friend in the Fitzgerald group, standing next to her mother, Grace. Our eyes met, and I immediately said to my mother:

"Come on, there's Scar." With my arms linked with my father's, we made our way over.

Mom was on the other side of Dad.

"Hello, darlings," Grace Fitzgerald immediately said, approaching with kisses on our cheeks.

All the Fitzgeralds were there, except for the president and the vice-president.

"How's life in Washington DC?" my father asked Arnold.

Mr. Arnold, Scarlett's father, had once been our president. He was now retired but still involved in politics, with his son being the vice-president and his nephew being the president.

I left them talking and moved to my friend's side, who took my hand and interlaced our fingers.

"Excited?" she asked in a whisper.

"Hoping I won't have to keep company with some old man," I murmured, knowing that sometimes we were auctioned off to elderly men who just wanted our company for dinner, feeling younger in the process.

"At least you have that hope. I know I'll be bid on by Sawyer; I heard my father asking him for that." Scar sighed, her shoulders slumping.

"I'd love to be bid on by Sawyer just to make my governor jealous," I teased, seeing my friend shake her head.

"You're hopeless, Zozo." She controlled herself to avoid bursting into laughter.

Sawyer was William's younger brother. He was tall, like all the Fitzgeralds, but there was a contrast in him that the others didn't have. A bit of a bad boy, he usually rode his motorcycle. He had a law degree. For someone used to seeing all the Fitzgeralds neatly dressed in suits, Sawyer often wore tight jeans, combat boots, and tousled brown hair.

If it weren't for events like this one, or even on those occasions, he managed to be the different one. Walking alongside the governor, I saw him approaching in dress pants and shoes. He wore a button-down shirt over his pants, with the top buttons undone, revealing tattoos on his chest.

But my focus wasn't on him; it was on the impeccably dressed governor next to him. His striking blue eyes, hair neatly combed to the side, locked onto mine for the usual amount of time, and then quickly diverted to his family as he approached them.

"Look who's arrived," Scar whispered to me with a mocking tone.

"A feast for my eyes." I sighed, knowing that tonight would be just another of the many nights the governor would ignore me.

Abigail, approaching the group, immediately hugged her two sons, who looked at her with disdain.

For men, that was usually torture.

"I heard Mrs. Enoch is telling everyone she wants to bid on Will," Scar whispered in my ear.

"I hope so; he needs someone like Angélica in his life..."

"You know she wants something more with him." My friend looked at me, puzzled.

"She might want that, but William doesn't go for women from these events unless they're models." I rolled my eyes.

"Sometimes I'm startled by how much you know about my cousin." Scarlett widened her eyes.

"It's just observations." I smiled, turning my gaze forward, locking eyes with William. That look was new to me; after all, he never looked at others when talking to someone.

I held his gaze, not backing down, challenging him to see who would look away first, and of course, it was him, as someone called for him.

My whole body felt warm; my cheeks must have turned red. As William managed to remain unnoticed, no one even noticed our exchanged glances.

"It's about to start," Abigail announced, looking at me and Scarlett. "We'll begin with the women first."

Most of the women being auctioned were young, daughters of businessmen, all dreaming of being bid on by someone on the level of the Fitzgeralds.

For me, it was something completely out of reality, given that Malcolm would never allow a meeting with the governor. That loyalty among men irritated me to extreme levels.

I followed Abigail, and we met some of the young women; in total, there were five of us, with one not really counting since Scar would be bid on by her own cousin. Her presence there was just to show that there was a woman from the governor's family, a man everyone respected. If only they knew it was all just a facade.

CHAPTER TEN

William

Malcolm must have been crazy; what he asked of me was sheer madness. Sure, we were friends, and bidding on his sister wouldn't cause any discomfort among the guests since I had a fiancée. Zoey always stayed within my family's circle.

"What's the problem, little brother?" Sawyer sat down next to me as the girls took their places on the stage.

"This whole thing is a problem; I don't know why I agreed to this," I grumbled, irritated.

"Abigail, that's why we agreed," my brother stated the obvious.

"And if that wasn't enough, Malcolm asked me to bid on his sister," I retorted, finding yet another reason for this madness.

"That girl is going to rope you in someday." I rolled my eyes at Sawyer's comment.

"I'd like to see you with a woman like that on your tail."

"Let's face it, she's quite the problem, and a beautiful one at that." Sawyer continued to scrutinize Zoey on stage.

"Keep your eyes off her; she's Malcolm's sister," I ordered, reprimanding him.

"Admit that you love the way that little girl is on your case." I glared at his mocking eyes.

"Zoey is Malcolm's sister and always will be, even though she's become a very beautiful woman; she'll always be Malcolm's sister. My friendship with him is worth more than his bratty little sister." I shrugged, grabbing the whiskey glass from the table.

"So what's the problem with bidding on her?" Obviously, Sawyer wasn't going to let go of his teasing.

I didn't answer him, keeping my eyes on the stage. I focused on the girl in the middle; she was the shortest of them all, wearing a moss-green dress, her long, wavy hair cascading over her shoulders, gently brushing against the beautifully shaped neckline.

Zoey wore high heels that were visible when she walked, showcasing her lovely legs through the side slit of her dress.

Our eyes met again, and once more, the little schemer caught me in the act of scrutinizing her. This was wrong, way too wrong!

The auction started with a young woman; the initial bids were low, but soon they increased to a higher amount, until she was won by an older gentleman. That was typical of those men; they just wanted the company of the girl for a dinner, to feel young again.

My mother was grateful for the amount, which always helped the organizations supported by her club.

The second girl was auctioned off for a price similar to the first. Then it was Zoey Beaumont's turn. The person at the microphone was one of the men working for my mother.

"Our third young lady is Zoey Beaumont, a sweet girl who enjoys chatting," it was evident from Zoey's look that she hated the way she was introduced.

The bids began, and I remained alert to see who was raising their paddle. If it were those older gentlemen, I wouldn't even care, but my problem started when Louis Newton began bidding, competing with Jared Lins, an older businessman.

The amount kept rising as both raised their paddles; Jared's forehead grew even more wrinkled. He was going to stop bidding. Louis couldn't win; he was young and might try too much with Zoey. Malcolm would be angry with me. *Damn*!

I wanted to be closer to Jared to keep him bidding, but the old man was about to stop.

"Is that it? No more bids? Will Miss Beaumont be won by the young man in the red shirt?" The auctioneer, behind the microphone, was asking for more bids.

My eyes went to my paddle; I picked it up, knowing I would need to raise it. It was just an auction; there was no need to actually go out with Zoey. I'd do it for Malcolm. *Oh, if he only knew what I briefly considered doing with his sister.*

"Anyone else?" The auctioneer's voice echoed in my mind.

Without thinking, I raised my paddle and offered an exorbitant amount to ensure no one else bid on that woman.

The entire hall fell silent. My eyes fixed on Zoey, who narrowed hers, knowing that I did it to prevent her from going out with Louis.

They asked two more times if anyone had another bid, but when no one did, the gavel came down, and I had won the bid for little Beaumont, my small torment.

The fourth girl's turn came; the previously auctioned girls were leaving from the side. Zoey maintained her delicate smile, but it was clear she disapproved of my intention.

Behind the tables, where I was alone with my brother, I could hear her soft footsteps approaching me without even looking at her.

Her body stopped behind my chair; I kept my gaze fixed on the stage, knowing that the last one would be my cousin.

"You had no right!" she huffed, murmuring angrily behind me. "I'm talking to you, Mr. Fitzgerald!"

She stamped her foot, and I was forced to lift my face, seeing that she might be about to put on one of her little shows.

"This is an auction, and I can do whatever I want if I have the money to pay for it." I gave a small, mocking smile.

"You did it because my brother asked; of course, you don't want this dinner with me. You took away the chance for me to have a moment like this!" She widened her black eyes at me.

"You wanted a dinner with Mr. Newton? He's not worth all this effort." I shrugged.

"What's not worth it is you! You had no right; it was my dinner, and you took it from me." Zoey threw her long black hair back, exposing her neckline even more. Her medium-sized breasts were round, and I could cover them with my entire hand.

"Just know that I'll tell everyone about the fraud that you are." I knew the little one was bluffing. Her anger was speaking louder; she didn't want to be left on the losing end, making her fury evident.

How did Zoey know about my staged engagement? How did that little thing know so much about me?

I turned my face and looked at my brother.

"Don't let anyone bid on Scar," I ordered, protecting my only female cousin.

"Don't worry, go take care of your tornado before it tears everything apart," my brother mocked.

"She's not mine," I muttered, standing up from my chair. I put my hand on Zoey's wrist, and while no one was watching, I pulled her along with me.

"Where do you think you're taking me?" She tried to pull her arm away, but I didn't let her go and brought her with me.

It was clearly obvious that Zoey wasn't coming willingly.

CHAPTER ELEVEN

Zoey

"What do you think you're doing?" I tried to pull my arm away again when William brought me to a private room in the hall.

He released my arm, and a light turned on, filling the room with an orange glow that made it look like an office.

"You're not going to say anything, understood?" His voice was dominated by that possessive tone.

"Who's going to stop me, you?" I mocked, crossing my arms. "And besides, don't you ever pull my arm like that again!"

A pout formed on my lips.

"Do you think you can blackmail me? I could tell your brother everything about you, and fuck what I told you," he growled, advancing towards me until my backside hit the edge of the desk.

I widened my eyes, my fingers gripping the mahogany desk behind me.

"So go ahead and tell him. Let's see what Malcolm thinks about his best friend wanting to punish his sister." I raised an eyebrow, defiant despite my fear.

"Wasn't it you who wanted to be punished?" The governor stopped in front of me, his hands resting on the desk as he leaned over my body.

"I want you to go to hell for what you did!" I didn't look away.

"Has anyone ever told you that you're very petulant?"

"They can say whatever they want about me, but I won't let anyone interfere with my dinner." William pursed his lips, setting them in a straight line.

"You wanted to be with that man?" His voice was low, almost hoarse and dominating.

"Yes, I did." Our eyes locked and didn't waver.

"And why would you want a dinner with him and not with me?" A brief smile formed on my lips.

"Louis isn't my brother's friend, Louis wouldn't bid on me and give me the dinner back. I know you'll never have dinner with me," I declared without hesitation, venting my frustration.

"Who guarantees that?" The governor's face slowly moved closer to mine, like a predator about to strike.

"I do." I exhaled in a whisper.

"Well, you're right. I don't dine with petulant women..."

"Only with those who have engagement contracts?" I cut him off, showing that I wouldn't be intimidated by his attempt at punishment.

William snarled, a rough growl I had never heard from him before. He gripped my waist and effortlessly turned me around, as if I were a rag doll. His large hand pressed against my back, pushing me so that my rear was sticking out.

"I hate, I despise being defied." I tried to grab onto something, but as if he was used to this, the governor held my wrists with one hand while the other pressed against my back, leaving my rear fully exposed.

"What do you think you're doing? I'll scream!" From my side, I could see the governor's face analyzing my rear.

"You little she-devil," he grunted, running his hand over the fabric of my dress and lifting it to expose my backside to him. "I'd like to smack that ass so hard that the next day all you'd remember is the sting of my spanks when you sit down..."

"Go ahead, governor," I taunted him fearlessly. "Hit me and see how much you'll regret it later. Hit me and watch the governor of California lamenting for trying to punish his best friend's sister."

William's eyes rose to mine, narrowing.

"You know I'm giving in to your blackmail, you know my body is starting to crave yours, and you know this is a mistake, and know..." His eyes roamed over my body, settling on my rear which I could feel shivering under his gaze. "That if I ever fuck your pussy, it will be my way, it will be because I couldn't hold back any longer, and it will happen in a way you'll never forget the cock that took you!"

With his free hand, I felt his fingers circling the edge of my panties, pulling them hard and tearing the small fabric, which he held up to his face, smelling the little lace.

"I'd rather have the scent of your honey on my nose than know I didn't fight my instinct to fuck you here and now," he growled, pocketing the fabric.

William released my wrists and I quickly stood up, our eyes meeting.

"If I see you looking at or talking to that Louis, I'll add another sentence to your notebook for when I can no longer hold back."

"Was that a threat? If it was, you'll need much more than that to stop me." I adjusted my dress and ran my fingers through my hair, making it clear that I was fixing it.

"Don't play with me, Zoey," he concluded in a whisper.

"Don't think you're dealing with one of your submissive conquests. I can be your biggest hell, governor. Don't try to mark your territory where it doesn't belong." I began walking towards the door.

His hands grabbed my wrist, preventing me from walking.

"I'll mark my territory wherever I want, and if I want, I'll plant a big flag on top of you, claiming you as mine!" His face moved closer to mine.

"Just don't forget about your fake fiancée." I did the same.

William released my wrist when we heard his name called over the microphone from outside.

"Behave, Zoey, if you don't want to be punished," he said, adjusting his suit as he headed towards the door.

William left, leaving me alone. My body was tense, my breathing heavy, and the spot between my legs was so damp that I could swear the honey was dripping down my thighs.

I exhaled heavily, recalling the governor's gaze on my rear and the way he desired me there, how he struggled against his instincts, making me realize that I had him. That man could be mine, even if it meant through provocation; William would be in my bed.

Regaining my composure as I realized I was alone, I gathered all my dignity and left the office. I needed a glass of champagne, and if I could find Louis, it would be even better to provoke jealousy in a possessive governor.

CHAPTER TWELVE

Zoey

I couldn't miss the governor's auction, enjoying watching the ladies go crazy trying to win a dinner with William Fitzgerald.

Scarlett had a huge pout on her lips; my friend was once again won by a man from her family.

"You know what I don't understand? Why do they send me to these auctions if I'm always won by someone from my family?" Scar complained, her eyes fixed on the stage as she watched William being won by a lady who even jumped with satisfaction.

"I've given up trying to understand the men in your family," I whispered, focusing my attention on William as he descended the side of the stairs with that scowl of his.

It was clear that most of the men present were not pleased; they were doing it because they were compelled by some family member, to help with the organization. Unlike us women, who loved all of it. All that little show of glances in our direction.

William turned to his family circle as soft music began to play once the auction ended, and from the corner of my eye, I spotted Louis approaching.

"Friend, my almost-buyer is coming," I whispered to Scarlett, who turned in her chair to adjust her posture.

"Hello, girls," Louis Newton immediately said, pulling up a chair without even asking if he could sit.

We both nodded our heads, watching him position himself next to us, clearly wanting something.

"It's a shame I didn't get my dinner." He directed his gaze at me.

"William thinks he has some power over me just because he's my brother's friend," I said directly, smiling to make it clear that it was all just the governor's game.

"Someone needs to remind our governor that he has a fiancée." Louis flashed a big smile, playing with the button on his sleeve.

"I thought I was the only one who thought that way." I raised my eyes, seeing the governor in the distance with a furrowed brow in my direction, and I could swear he was angry. I smiled at Louis.

"Is there any other way to get a dinner with you besides being won at an auction?" Louis didn't take the smile off his face, making his charm and desire to take me out to dinner evident.

I reached for my handbag, opened it, and took out my phone.

"You can give me your number, and we'll discuss the best day." I handed him my phone with the keypad open so he could just enter his number.

We'd see how much of what the governor said was true.

Satisfied, Louis handed the phone back to me, leaning in slowly to give me a kiss on the cheek. He was a handsome man, but nothing compared to my governor. Still, I would do anything to cause a little hell in William's life.

"See you soon, then." Louis stood up from the chair, winking, and walked away.

"Wow, he was pretty straightforward," Scarlett whispered next to me.

"At least it served to make my governor jealous." I turned my face, smiling at my friend.

"I saw you two sneaking away from the edge of the hall. Are you going to tell me what happened, or do I need to pry information out of you?" Scar rolled her eyes as if I should have already told her where I went.

"I can't tell you here." I brought my mouth close to her ear. "I'm not wearing underwear; your cousin tore it..."

Scarlett pulled back and looked at me with wide eyes.

"It's not what you're thinking, but it's close," I murmured, not wanting anyone to overhear us.

"Oh God! What happened? I'm curious now," Scar said, leaning closer for me to tell her more.

"*Shh*, we can't risk being caught, but one thing I can guarantee is that I was right; I always am." I flashed my best confident smile. "The engagement is fake."

"Did he admit it?"

"He tried to make a move on me. What kind of engagement is that?"

"He wouldn't cross any lines with you if it were real, would he?" We didn't mention the governor's name to avoid the risk of being overheard.

"We know he wouldn't." We both smiled maliciously.

We spent the rest of the event gossiping about Scarlett's college adventures, not mentioning William again, as we were afraid someone might overhear us.

I could feel the governor's gaze on me the entire time, as if he was trying to uncover what I was discussing with Scar.

I APPROACHED MY PARENTS, who were standing next to Abigail and Edward, William's parents. My friend had just said goodbye, as she needed to return to her college the next day.

"Have you already set the date for the dinner?" Abigail asked as I stopped next to my mother.

"William did that just to help his friend." I rolled my eyes and crossed my arms.

"Oh, dear," Abigail scolded her son.

"Malcolm asked, and I just did it." The governor shrugged his shoulders.

"I have my perfect revenge with Mrs. Donnell who won him," I said with a touch of sarcasm, knowing that the widow loved to chat, and we all knew how much William hated that.

"No, no..." Abigail shook her head in disagreement. "You need to have dinner; we need to prove that these auctions aren't a scam."

"Why don't you put pressure on Sawyer like you are on me?" William retorted to his mother.

"Your brother can prove that he had dinner with Scarlett at any family dinner," Abigail said, always helping me side with her son whenever she had the chance.

I believed she was the only one helping me with the *governor*.

"It's just a joke. Invite Zoey to a family dinner, and it will all be resolved." I stared at William, narrowing my eyes.

"Family is perfect. Let me have dinner alone with Louis Newton; after all, he doesn't see any problem with my company." I gave a sarcastic smile.

"What's this about?" my father asked, making me look at him.

"Just a dinner, Dad." I blinked my eyes, trying to show how good I was as a daughter.

"That's perfect, dear; he's a good man." Abigail played along with me, clearly noticing how much her son disliked that. "We can schedule a dinner at my house; I love your company."

William cleared his throat, but given the circumstances, he ended up not saying anything. And if he had spoken, it would have been clear how much he cared about my dinner with Louis.

CHAPTER THIRTEEN

Zoey

My phone buzzed on the small table beside the stool, and I diverted my eyes from the screen where I was painting. Seeing the unknown number with a message:

"If you know it's with Newton, you can consider it another punishment I'll give you..."

I didn't need to be a mind reader to know who that message was from.

I grabbed my cloth beside the phone, leaving the brush in the holder, wiped my fingers, picked up my phone, and opened the message. As soon as I opened it, the governor's private number appeared. Only those closest to him had that number, and he had messaged me from it, causing my inner goddess to scream.

Before replying, I opened the profile picture, savoring the image of William in his typical suit, his dominant eyes; even his personal number had that imposing governor photo.

I returned to the chat and started typing:

"Too late, I've already set it up."

Which was a lie, I hadn't even talked to Louis yet, knew nothing about him. Since I was the only one with his number, he hadn't sent me a message.

"Do you think I'm joking?"

I hadn't even finished my thought when another message from him came through. William was such an easy man to rile up; I was enjoying this new side of him.

"I love playing games, we could do a few..."

I bit the corner of my lip, waiting for his response, but it didn't come. I waited for another two minutes, and when I still didn't get a reply, I returned my attention to my screen.

The night before, William hadn't spoken to me again, always directing his looks in a way that made it clear I should obey his orders.

I lost myself in my drawing, a green mountain with its peak reflecting a sunset. A new technique I needed to practice for my art course.

I was so absorbed in my drawing that I barely noticed my phone vibrating non-stop, with several messages, one after the other.

I picked up the phone, seeing William send exclamation points just to get my attention. I opened the message, a smile spreading across my lips. It was so like him. Always wanting everything *yesterday.*

"Why the hell aren't you responding?"

I read the message with his tone echoing in my mind, full of his possessiveness.

"Not everything revolves around you, governor. I'm very busy."

I sent the message, analyzing my painting and thinking about which color to use next. Before I could return to my painting, my phone buzzed again.

"What's more important than me?"

I read the message and quickly sent another:

"You're so full of yourself; there are many things more important than you..."

I left the message open, just to plant the seed of doubt in his mind.

"What are you doing, Miss Beaumont?"

I was wondering how he had gotten my number and what the hell the governor wanted with me.

"Why don't we get straight to the point? What do you want from me?"
I didn't answer his question. I didn't want to be the one to give all the information while he revealed nothing.

William's message didn't come immediately like the others. Was the conversation over? Did he just want to mark his territory and see if I would go out with Louis?

"I want my dinner, but in return, you won't go out with Louis."

His message caught me off guard; I hadn't expected that. I didn't imagine he would demand his dinner. I bit the corner of my lip, my inner devil letting out a devilish giggle.

Did he think it would be that easy?

"Dear governor, too late. I'm going out with Louis tonight."

I hoped he would believe my lie.

"You've always wanted my fucking attention, and now that you have it, you're playing games? I'll give you just one chance; if you don't take it, there won't be another..."

That message made me anxious. William wasn't the type of man to insist on something for too long, and now he was asking me to dinner. This would likely be my only chance.

"Just because you said I'm playing hard to get, I'm refusing your invitation."

I hoped I wouldn't regret what I had sent. This was the chance I had always wanted, and now I was wasting it.

William hadn't replied; he wasn't going to. I turned my eyes back to my screen, maybe I should return to painting since I had thrown away my only chance to be with the man I had dreamed about since childhood.

"I want you in my apartment, today, at 8 PM. And if you're not there, I swear on everything sacred, I'll fuck you so hard you'll forget your own name!"

That message was like balm for my eyes. William hadn't given up; he had just issued a command. He wanted me there. What the governor wanted from me, I still didn't know. But something inside me screamed that this man was falling for all my advances.

"*Governor... governor... try your luck...*"

It was obvious that message made me curious, and my curiosity was strong enough to make me want to go to the governor's place and see what awaited me.

Going to a man's apartment wasn't exactly my usual thing, but William felt like family, a family without blood ties. After all, I wanted him, I longed to trace my tongue over his chest just to taste him.

I might arrive a little late; a bit of drama would do him good. But first, I needed to think about what to wear and if the lingerie I had at home was good enough for if we decided to take things further.

It would be a real Godsend.

William hadn't sent me anything else; he had probably figured out that he shouldn't always believe what I said. After all, when it came to me, I liked a bit of flirting and playing hard to get, even if the subject was him.

The man I desired most in my life.

CHAPTER FOURTEEN

William

Maybe I should be grateful that little troublemaker didn't show up. What was she thinking, inviting my best friend's sister to my penthouse?

I circled the whiskey glass with my finger.

Since I allowed that little tornado to enter my life, it's as if I haven't had a sober day. Her dark eyes always wandering through my thoughts, the way she always tries to get my attention, challenging me.

This had never happened before; all the women I dealt with were submissive. Zoey confronted me, with all her lively spirit, making me want her to be mine...

Mine for just one night, at least that's what I had convinced myself.

I sat in my armchair and rested my arm on the backrest, with my whiskey glass there. Even if Zoey came here, explicitly no one would suspect anything since she was my best friend's sister and my cousin's friend. It was as if we were all part of the same family, the same social circle.

I took the last sip from my glass. I checked my watch and saw it was 9 PM; that was definitive. She wasn't coming. Had she gone to that damn dinner with Newton?

I expected everything from Zoey, except that the girl who always seemed to be in love with me would change her mind.

Hell! I shouldn't be thinking about a girl who wasn't meant for me, who couldn't under any circumstances be mine. I got up from the chair, my breathing becoming heavy, *damn it*! I was jealous of that damn girl.

The doorbell rang, and I was surprised; I hadn't ordered anything, nor had I called any girl to come over. I headed to the elevator. My penthouse had a private elevator, and when someone arrived, they either rang the bell or entered the code. Since only those I had authorized could come up, it had to be someone from my family.

I unlocked the door to open it. My eyes focused on the girl who was there, *damn it! She came!*

"What are you doing here?" I said as the sound of her heels echoed on the floor, following her movements with my eyes.

"Do I need to show you our messages? Or are you going to tell me that wasn't you?" Zoey rolled her eyes in my direction.

She was wearing a white denim skirt that reached mid-thigh and a top that exposed one of her shoulders, a fabric that didn't accentuate her curves.

"Yes, but the arrangement was for an hour ago." I put my hand in my pocket.

"Women are always late." Zoey shook her head, looking around. "I think the last time I was here, the sofa wasn't this color..."

Her comment died, disregarding my reprimand as she headed towards the sofa.

"Women who go out with me never show up late," I declared as Zoey sat on the sofa and crossed her legs, revealing her tanned skin.

"Good thing I'm not one of the women who go out with you. After all, do you have anything to eat? I'm hungry; did you invite me here for tea?"

Maybe I wasn't prepared for that level of Zoey Beaumont, but she had come, even if late, she had come to the lion's den, and didn't even seem scared.

"Everything I bought has gone cold." I shrugged.

"So you bought something?" Zoey's eyes lit up slightly.

She tried to act like a strong woman, but deep down, she always showed her true essence as a charming girl.

"If you had come an hour ago..."

"I was very busy with my dinner..." My eyes narrowed as I looked at hers.

"Were you with another man before coming here?" My voice came out as a whisper, my hands clenching into fists.

"Yes, why?" She stood up from the sofa, adjusting her skirt and lifting her face towards mine. "A woman always needs two options."

She smiled shamelessly, walking slowly towards where I was standing.

"Not mine," I growled without thinking.

"I'm not yours; after all, you have a fiancée." Zoey shook her head, clearly saying that to provoke me.

"How do you know?" I asked as she passed by me, heading into the kitchen.

Zoey had been here once with her brother, so she knew most of the rooms in the penthouse.

"About your fake engagement?" she asked, examining the untouched plates of food I had ordered from my favorite restaurant.

"Yes."

"I just know," again she didn't answer my question.

"You're the only one who comes up with this theory. What's the reason behind it?" Zoey, who was standing by my kitchen island, raised her eyes towards me.

"Well, it's not just based on you, but on all the Fitzgeralds. You're not the type of man who lets his fiancée go out, travel far without being together; you're too jealous to allow such a thing. Zachary doesn't let Savannah set foot outside the house without knowing where she's going. Christopher was once married, and everyone saw that they were always together, not to mention your parents' and uncles' relationships.

It's easy to judge that your engagement is fake; you don't even care about her." Zoey turned her gaze back to the plates, removing the cover without even asking if she could eat.

"I might not be like them," I retorted.

"That's a distinctive trait of yours; I doubt it's not." She shrugged. "Your engagement is fake, just confirm it for me to make sure I was always right. You know I can keep a secret."

She gave a side smile, the kind she always used to give her father or brother when she wanted something.

"Just tell me if it was really at that dinner?" I put my hand in my pants pocket as Zoey pulled out the stool and sat down, leaning on the footrest.

"I'm starving. Clearly, I didn't go. Who goes to a dinner and comes back hungry?"

Zoey was more observant than I had imagined; I hadn't even considered that resemblance between me and my family.

I had never had a real woman, one I wanted to live by my side. I knew what family love was, after all, I loved my parents..., but a woman? I didn't know what that feeling was, I had never loved anyone, never had anyone make me want to be better for another person.

"Now you owe me my answer." Zoey broke into my thoughts.

"Maybe I'll give it later." I gave a brief smile, watching her frown and make that disgusted face.

I walked towards the stool in front of Zoey, pulling it out.

CHAPTER FIFTEEN

Zoey

The governor was sitting right in front of me, and I had given him the information he wanted, but William hadn't answered what I wanted to know.

"Is there anything for dessert?" I asked, bringing the fork to my mouth, brushing my lips against it.

"It depends." The governor set his fork down on his side of the table.

"What do you mean?" I asked, playing along with his game.

"Do you want to be my chocolate sauce?" William let his eyes drift over the fabric of my shirt, but there was nothing for him to see since I was wearing a loose shirt with no cleavage, completely covering my breasts.

"I don't like chocolate." I shrugged, returning the fork to my mouth.

"Who doesn't like chocolate?" He raised an eyebrow in an amusing way.

"Those who prefer strawberry?" After finishing my plate of food, I set my fork aside.

"But let's face it, chocolate is way better than strawberry." The governor got up from his stool, and my eyes followed his movements.

"I disagree, strawberry is better in every way." I bit the corner of my lip as he opened the fridge, expecting him to grab a dessert, but instead, he pulled out a champagne glass.

He set the two frosted glasses on the counter and took a champagne bottle from a shelf that I hadn't seen before.

"Strawberry is good as a fruit, but it doesn't compare to chocolate." He opened the bottle with ease.

"You could have mentioned you had this champagne earlier," I grumbled as I watched him fill the glasses.

"I didn't want you to drink alcohol before eating." The governor handed me one of the glasses.

"So considerate," I declared, rolling my eyes and taking the glass he offered.

"Does anyone know you're here?" he asked, stopping in front of me as our eyes met when I lifted my face.

"Just my entire family." I gave a smirking smile.

"Liar," he retorted.

"Of course, no one knows I'm here. Can you imagine what they'd think?"

"Well, are you here to declare your feelings to me again?" His voice had a hint of mischief.

I brought the champagne to my lips, taking a small sip. Without breaking eye contact, William looked away, heading towards the living room.

Holding the glass in my fingers, I got off the stool and followed the governor, watching him sit in his armchair with his legs crossed, while he lifted his gaze towards me.

"Is there something between you and Louis Newton?" he asked, moistening his lips as he finished speaking.

"You didn't answer my question, so I'm not going to answer yours." I shrugged and walked over to his sofa, where I sat and crossed my legs.

"You already know the answer to my question," he said as I took another small sip of the delicious champagne.

"I want to hear the answer from your lips." I gave a brief smile.

"My engagement is a sham, are you happy now?" He rested his arm on the back of his chair, not taking his eyes off mine.

"Very satisfied, to tell the truth. But I'm not ready to answer your question." I bit the corner of my lip, watching the governor let out a slight sigh of frustration. "Unless..."

I didn't finish my sentence, adding a bit of drama, and William showed signs of impatience.

"Unless you admit you want something with me," I finished, as he seemed too impatient to continue with anything.

"That's obvious, but I still have my doubts." William ran his hand over his beard, his fingers grazing the stubble as if he were thinking about it.

My eyes wandered around his penthouse. I dreamed of the possibility of someday being here, being his, having the freedom to come and go as if we could be a couple.

"Is Malcolm your doubt?" I broke the silence by asking him.

"I can't break the number one rule of our friendship," he declared.

"But I'm here now," I whispered, gently running my tongue over my lip.

"Yes, you are, and we might be making a serious mistake," he said, watching me get up from the sofa where I had been sitting.

"What mistakes, exactly?" I asked playfully, setting the glass on the coffee table and walking toward my governor.

"Zoey... Zoey... you shouldn't have accepted my invitation. You should have stayed far away from me," he said, focusing his attention on the center of my belly.

"I like danger, I like pushing boundaries," I whispered, taking a small step to stand between his legs.

"Do you really?" the governor murmured, his voice rough.

I simply nodded as he moved, placed the glass on the side table next to his armchair, and quickly grasped my waist, pressing his face against the middle of my belly.

When he lifted the fabric, I felt William's beard graze my skin. I tightened my hands by my sides as a squeal escaped from deep in my throat when I felt him bite my belly. I raised my hand impulsively, trying to push him away, but the governor wouldn't let me move and pressed me harder with his fingers.

"Did you really think it would be that easy?" he whispered, blowing on the skin he had just bitten.

I was about to respond when his phone rang. William pulled the device from his pocket.

"Damn it," he murmured, turning the device to show my brother's name on it. "I need to answer this, stay silent."

I merely nodded, watching him answer the call. I stepped away from the governor, keeping a few inches between us.

"When, now?" William even seemed to gasp during the call.

I didn't know what they were talking about, so I waited impatiently for some response from him until the governor ended the call.

"I have to go," he said, putting the phone away.

"I have to?" I widened my eyes.

"Yes, your brother is coming with the helicopter. We have matters to resolve, and it seems to be extremely urgent." William nodded towards the door for me to follow him.

I slumped my shoulders, heading towards the elevator door. William pressed the button, and I waited for the doors to open.

"Seems like it was a sign," he said, looking up at me.

"A sign?" I rolled my eyes at his conversation. "Keep your signs, I'm going home..."

I walked past him, about to enter the elevator when William grabbed my wrist, pulling me close, and I held onto his shirt to keep my balance.

"We can't, Zoey, this is a mistake," he said, holding my chin, "but I don't want to give up on you..."

His face leaned towards mine, giving me a prolonged peck, not deepening the kiss, just something soft.

"What do you want, governor?" I asked, closing and opening my eyes slowly.

"Right now, I want you, but we can't do this now. Your brother is about to arrive," William released me, I took a step back, and the doors were already open for me.

With a long sigh, I stepped in. My eyes met William's as the doors closed, hoping this wasn't the end for us.

CHAPTER SIXTEEN

Zoey

I could distinguish my brother's voice when I woke up that morning, talking downstairs at my parents' house.

Malcolm must have come to talk to William and took the opportunity to visit our parents. Slowly, I got out of bed, changed in the suite, putting on one of my leggings and a running top, since I always liked to go for a run in the morning before starting my painting.

I went to the suite to do everything I needed. I tied my hair and returned to my room, watching the door slowly open and noticing my brother's presence.

"Can I come in?" he asked, already entering my room. I just nodded; after all, I had already changed. "I talked to William about you..."

Without finishing the sentence, Malcolm made a face.

"You talked, did you?" I don't know why, but the fact that they had talked didn't surprise me at all. I very much doubt William said anything.

"He said that Louis Newton was talking to you. Is that right?" There was my protective brother.

"Yes, but it was nothing serious," I muttered, rolling my eyes. That was typical of William.

"I don't want these men marking territory on my sister," he said in his most controlling manner.

"Our dad saw it and didn't think it was a big deal," I declared, picking up my earbuds.

"Yes, because Dad never sees anything wrong," my brother continued.

"Malcolm, little brother." I stopped in front of him, giving my best smile. "Nothing happened. He gave me his number, and I didn't even call him back. Besides, I'm an adult; I know what to do with my life."

"You're only nineteen, to me that's still young enough," he continued talking until I affirmed that nothing would happen between me and Louis.

"You can relax, brother, nothing will happen," I hoped that speaking this way he would understand.

"Promise? I don't want any man touching my little sister," how to tell him that his "little sister" had already been used?

"Yes, Malcolm, but you need to understand that your little sister here has grown up and is plenty grown-up to learn to handle herself," I said, moving towards him.

I stood on the tips of my sneakers, placing my hand on Malcolm's shoulder and giving him a tight hug.

"Is that all you talked about regarding me?" I asked as I pulled away, seeing my brother shake his head.

"Zozo, William is and will never be good enough to be your man." He tried to mess up my hair, but I dodged him, heading towards the door.

"You know I've always been a dreamer," I declared a bit too loudly to be heard.

"Yes, and that's why you deserve a prince, not a frog like the friend whose character I know." I turned my face, seeing him watch me.

Like everyone else, Malcolm didn't take seriously what I felt for William. He thought his friend respected him enough not to make a move on me.

"Now he's engaged, so it will remain just a dream." My shoulders slumped.

Even if I dreamed, even if I idealized a moment, it would always be fleeting dreams. The world could end, and I could even have Abigail's help, but I would never have anything with the governor.

WILLIAM HADN'T RESPONDED to my messages anymore. When I sent the third one and saw that I wouldn't get a reply, I didn't insist. I knew I was persistent, but not a fool who would humiliate myself endlessly.

Seven days had passed since Malcolm was there, and something made the governor distance himself from me again.

Well, if he thought I would be crying over him, he was very, *very wrong*.

Scarlett was in the middle of exams, so I needed to rely on my nearby friends.

A new nightclub was having its grand opening, so I just told my parents I was going to spend the night at a friend's house. After all, I had spent the week working on a new painting and hadn't finished the details yet, not to mention the prep course that was draining my soul.

I was tired of staying at home; all I needed was a party, plenty of booze, and dancing.

Maybe cry a little over nearly having the governor and losing him. All thanks to my beloved brother. Malcolm would always be our barrier.

"HEY, FRIEND," KATY called out over the music.

I turned my face and waited for her to speak, making it clear that I was listening to what she had to say.

"Let's go to the bar, do you want to come with me?"

I just nodded, dripping with sweat from dancing. None of those men caught my attention; none had the presence or the strong hands of my governor.

I made my way through the crowd, getting stepped on and jostled, which made me complain several times.

Katy ordered double shots of tequila; after all, the goal of the night was to forget our names.

If Scarlett were here, she'd be scolding me for putting up with this.

I downed the entire glass, grimacing as I sucked on the lime. Shortly after, we went back to the center of the dance floor and stayed near the table where we had been. There were a lot of people, but none I clearly knew, maybe just by sight.

I had only one true friend, Scar. The rest were just acquaintances—people I could rely on only for parties, not for confiding secrets.

Several sweet drink glasses were handed to me. They must have been some kind of liquor; since we were in the VIP area, the drinks were served directly to us.

I didn't even find Katy again; we had met at the prep course we attended together.

The last time I saw her, she had her tongue in some guy's mouth. They must have been off somewhere getting hot and heavy. I was envious of her, as I was so drunk I couldn't see anything clearly in front of me.

"Miss Beaumont?" a male voice reverberated in my ear, gripping my arm a bit tighter.

"Hey," I complained, turning around. I blinked several times, trying to see if I knew the man spinning right in front of me.

"Come on, Mr. Fitzgerald is waiting for you." He literally pulled me along.

"Hey!" I complained a bit louder.

What the hell was this Fitzgerald guy talking about?

"I want to stay, let me go," I grumbled, but no one cared that I was being dragged. "My bag..."

At my request, the man who looked more like a wardrobe than a person led me to the counter where our belongings were kept.

"Who are you?" I asked, knowing this had to be something my father or brother arranged.

Of course, I didn't get an answer and was treated like a doll as I continued to be dragged along.

CHAPTER SEVENTEEN

William

I still couldn't believe I was subjecting myself to this, waiting for my driver to return with that crazy woman.

Malcolm asked me to pick up Zoey because her parents were away on a trip and couldn't get her from the club, where she clearly shouldn't have been. I had to remind my friend that she was already an adult and could do whatever she wanted.

He took the opportunity to mention my cousin Scarlett, and of course, I would do anything for her. Scar was our girl; we watched her grow up, followed my aunt's high-risk pregnancy, so it was as if she were the sister of all our cousins.

But with Zoey, it was different. I still had that damn thong under my pillow, feeling it between my fingers as if I were touching it.

I wanted and desired that little whirlwind.

I shouldn't have been here, but look where I was—right where I'd most tried to avoid, next to that cheeky little thing.

Through the window, I saw Malcolm's sister coming out of the club. Yes, that's how I'd refer to her, *as Malcolm's sister*, that way I'd be reminded of his name every time.

Zoey was practically being carried by my bodyguard, with her purse in his hand, and the girl seemed to complain with every step she took.

My other bodyguard opened the door as they approached, and the cold night air touched my body. How could that crazy woman wear that tiny dress?

"No, you don't control me," I heard her say with a slurred voice.

"Just let her in," I said authoritatively. Of course, my bodyguard didn't throw her in but forced her inside, where she sat awkwardly.

"Let me go," she mumbled without lifting her face.

Zoey dropped her head between her legs, her long hair spread out.

"I wanted to have fun, annoying people," she mumbled, looking down.

The last thing I had planned for that night was dealing with a drunk woman.

"Let's go to my penthouse. I'm not leaving this girl alone in this state at her place," I declared to my driver.

God forgive me, but I was trying to stay strong.

Hearing my voice made Zoey lift her face. She had dark makeup that was still intact, and her red lips revealed her lipstick. What an extraordinarily beautiful girl. *Malcolm's sister...*

"My governor." Zoey gave a mischievous smile, trying to tuck her hair behind her ear in a failed attempt.

"Please, Miss Beaumont, have some manners," I asked, trying to be patient.

Fortunately, my penthouse was nearby, and we would be there soon.

"I could be Mrs. Fitzgerald," she pouted those slightly plump lips. "But you don't want that..."

Zoey lowered her face, and as if a gust of wind had hit her, she was thrown to the side—my side! Her face smashed into my leg, her hand gripping my thigh, a weak laugh escaping her mouth.

"So fragrant..." she mumbled, running her finger. "I could run all my fingers over your body..."

"Miss!" I scolded her, lifting her face, making her return to her place.

"Annoying, boring... loose ass..." she continued to throw words at me.

Luckily, the car entered the underground parking of my apartment. I would have thanked if I could, but I stayed silent. As soon as the car stopped, I got out first and went around. I easily picked up the small girl in my arms.

"Humm... big guy." Her hand squeezed my arm.

"Sir, here's her bag," the bodyguard said. I just nodded and took it.

Fortunately, due to the time, there were no residents around. I stopped in front of my elevator, calling it, and it quickly opened. I entered, entered the code so the doors would open as soon as we got upstairs.

"Can you stop touching my chest?" I asked, as Malcolm's sister's hands continued to move up, closer to my neck.

"Shut up, this is my dream," Zoey said with such conviction that it seemed she really was dreaming. "And in my dream, you're mine..."

Her daring hand continued to move across my chest, heading towards my neck again.

"The thing is, this isn't a dream. You're drunk, and you've crossed every line of sobriety." The doors opened, and we exited the elevator.

I went straight to my bedroom, the only one prepared for someone to sleep. I'd sort out one of the other rooms for myself later.

"You're so uptight even in my dreams." I pushed open my door with my foot.

I bumped the light switch with my elbow. I walked over to my bed and laid her down. I could give her a cold shower; it was what she deserved for letting herself get into that state. But I wouldn't do that because I wouldn't know how to deal with her wet body.

"At least your bed smells just like I always thought it would." She turned, hugging the pillow next to her.

Without even taking off her heels, she threw one leg over the other, revealing the curve of her ass. *Damn! She's Malcolm's sister...*

"My governor," she whispered, her voice almost a sigh.

Hell, what was wrong with that girl? Why this obsession with me? And damn it! I was starting to fall for her traps, wanting to hear that sweet little mouth teasing me, telling me how crazy she was about me.

I bent down near her feet, took off her shoe, and Zoey didn't even move, revealing she was asleep. She wore that tiny dress; I could change it, but I wasn't crazy enough to mess with Malcolm's sister's curves.

Even though we hadn't grown up together, since she was almost the same age as my cousin, I sometimes saw her at family parties, but we never had a long conversation. It was always in family groups. What did that cheeky little thing see in me to think of me as her prince?

With a heavy sigh, I took the blanket from the foot of the bed and draped it over her small body, covering her. Zoey mumbled something I didn't understand, hugged the pillow, snuggled up, and went back to sleep.

I stared at her for long minutes, went to the bedside lamp, left the dim light on, and walked to my closet, where I grabbed a change of clothes so I could shower in the other room.

I walked down the hallway, holding the clothes under my arm, and sent Malcolm a message letting him know that his sister was safe in my penthouse. I decided to bring her to my place because she was so drunk and I didn't want to leave her alone at home.

I was sure Malcolm would understand.

CHAPTER EIGHTEEN

Zoey

I twisted my lip with that piercing thump in my head; it felt like a little monkey banging cymbals in my brain. It hurt so much, and I placed my hand on my head, massaging my forehead.

Where the hell was I? How did I end up in a bed?

I lost track with the drinks. I took a deep breath and smelled that masculine essence invade my nostrils. Where was I? My eyes opened quickly, but they shut again because the brightness was too much.

I turned my face, dragging my nose against the pillow, *was I dreaming?* Or was that really Governor William's scent?

This time, my eyes opened slowly as I adjusted to the light and realized I wasn't dreaming; I was actually in the governor's bed, alone. If this were a dream, he'd be there with me. *Damn*, it was reality, I was in his bed. And I didn't even remember how the hell I got there.

I sat up in the bed, ran my hand through my hair, and looked around, confused by everything.

How? How? How?

That was all that echoed in my mind.

The door opened, and my eyes went to it, as if expecting anyone but him. Governor William.

"You're awake," he said. I lowered my head, expecting him to come with a grand lecture.

But nothing came. William stood at the door, as if waiting for a reaction from me. I couldn't even decipher how I ended up there, let alone say something.

Next to me, the bed didn't look messed up as if someone had slept there, so that meant the governor hadn't shared the bed with me.

"Aren't you going to say anything, Miss Beaumont?" After a long pause, he wanted to know.

"Can I leave?" I asked, feeling my head throbbing.

"You have a headache, don't you? That's why I won't give you a grand lecture now; it'd just go in one ear and out the other." I still kept my head down.

"Then I want to leave." All I wanted was to go, no lectures.

"There are pills for you by the bed." I turned my face and saw a glass and some pills. "Take them, and in an hour, come to the living room to talk. And please, take a shower."

Our eyes met.

"Shower where?" I asked, still confused.

"There." He pointed to his suite.

"In your bathroom?" I questioned, still baffled.

"Where else, silly?" He frowned.

"Oh..." I gasped, biting the corner of my lip.

"Well, I'm leaving. Just don't mess with my things." William cleared his throat, turned, and left the room.

I looked around for the first time alone in the governor's room. It could be a good reason to speculate about everything there. But it wasn't the best time. My head hurt, the moral hangover was hitting hard, and I still had to face the talk with the governor.

I placed my feet on the floor, took the pills, and swallowed them with the glass of water.

I got out of bed, adjusted my dress, and dragged my feet towards the suite. Maybe I was a bit curious to see where he showered. I pushed the door open, stopping in front of the mirror, and saw my pale reflection, dark circles under my eyes with smudged makeup.

Oh God! That was literally not the image I wanted William to see. After that, he would think Zoey was just a wreck.

I took off that dress smelling strongly of liquor. I left it on top of the toilet along with my lingerie. Without clothes, I walked to the glass shower and opened it.

There were his shampoos, all the items William used to bathe, right in front of me to use, smell, and appreciate.

I turned on the shower and put my fingers under the water to check the temperature until it was warm enough to wet myself.

I let the water fall over my head, allowing myself to wash my hair. My curious eyes picked up his shampoo, I opened the bottle, and held the scent near my nose, smelling the masculine aroma that reminded me so much of him.

I poured a little into my hand and worked it into my hair. I rubbed it slowly, wanting the scent to cling to my strands.

I left the shampoo in my hair, took his body wash, and scrubbed every part of my body, feeling the pain in my head slowly fade away.

I took my time in the shower, doing everything I could to prolong my encounter with William.

Once I was sure I was completely clean, I turned off the water, opened the glass door, stepped onto the mat, and reached for a white towel on the counter.

I dried my hair thoroughly, leaving it damp, and finally wrapped myself in the towel, exiting the bathroom with my hair still messy.

My eyes landed on some women's clothes on the bed, which was strange because they hadn't been there before. William must have left them. I approached and picked up the dress, noticing it still had the tag.

The fabric was a baby blue color. In a pink bag, there was something else; I opened it to find a white lingerie set, the fabric small and lacy. Delicate—had he helped pick it out?

I removed the towel from around my body, knowing no one was there. The panties fit perfectly, and the lace bra was also well-fitting; it had no padding but held my breasts nicely.

The dress was snug, especially around the bust, which was slightly loose due to the fabric's gathering. I left my hair on my shoulder, considering whether to sit on the bed and procrastinate a bit longer or to go downstairs and face the beast.

I knew William would talk about the club, how he must have found me—did he go inside? How did he get me out of there? Oh God, this was just getting worse.

I hoped that this incident hadn't made it to any sensationalist websites; my parents, who were traveling, would kill me.

Maybe it was time to face my greatest torment, confront the governor, and digest everything he had to say to me.

CHAPTER NINETEEN

Zoey

I bit the corner of my lip, descending one step at a time. My bare feet touched the ground as I dragged them.

My eyes focused on the man sitting in his armchair. He was looking at his phone, fiddling with something, not even glancing in my direction.

The governor was barefoot, wearing only a pair of sweatpants. He didn't look much like a man of power, but he still maintained his charm.

I approached him, and William put his phone down on the table beside the armchair. His eyes lifted in my direction, fingers intertwined over his crossed leg.

"Sit down." He pointed to the sofa.

I cleared my throat but ended up sitting, placing my hand on my legs that were exposed by the dress.

"Thank you for the clothes," I said, lifting my eyes to see him watching me.

"They look perfect on you"—the word *"perfect"* rolled off his lips in a sensual way.

I didn't say anything more, just waiting for him to start speaking.

"Aren't you going to say anything?" I asked, feeling restless.

"I don't see this as my problem," William said, letting his hands drop, and bringing one hand to his beard. "Or at least that's what I want to convince myself, but I'm deeply troubled by the way I found you yesterday."

"If it's something that doesn't concern you, you don't need to talk about it," I said, nervously fiddling with my fingers.

"Yes, it doesn't concern me, which makes me wonder if I should tell your brother or your father"—at that moment, I was scared; getting a lecture from two more men was too much.

This, compared to being 19 and still unable to live like an adult woman.

"You don't need to say anything. I won't do it again; I believe that's enough for you to know." I shrugged my shoulders, trying to appear indifferent.

"Zoey, what you don't understand is that the way I found you, any other man could have taken advantage of you. Imagine if you had woken up in any other bed but mine? Damn, you were so drunk that you just laid down in my bed and fell asleep. Do you realize the danger you put yourself in?" William kept his serious eyes on me, not diverting them. It wasn't just a reprimand; it was explicit concern.

I had nothing to say; I was in the wrong. I had put myself in danger, and it was all my fault.

"You know you're wrong, don't you?" William raised an eyebrow.

"Yes, I know," I murmured, looking down.

"I'm not going to play the role of a father, not that I see myself in that way," the governor declared, drawing my attention once more. "I just want you to promise me that you'll never do this again. Don't put yourself in such a situation."

What he was asking wasn't unreasonable; after all, I was embarrassed for myself.

"Yes, I promise." I moved my eyes towards the large glass wall, looking out at the city through it.

"Zoey?"—I loved the way he always called me, and our eyes met. "Now come here..."

I frowned, not understanding. Even though I was confused, I got up from the sofa. The governor raised his hand, making a gesture with his finger for me to come to him, and as if I were under a spell, I followed.

I stopped in front of the tall man. William leaned in, holding onto my waist.

"This is a mistake..."his voice trailed off, fingers pressing the fabric of the dress. "It's the first mistake I want to make."

I bit the corner of my lip, not quite understanding what he meant by that, or perhaps it was a part of me that still thought I might be dreaming.

"I think I'm still drunk," I murmured, dazed.

William pulled me in. It wasn't a casual pull but one with all the intention of making me sit on his lap. Each of my legs on either side of his thighs, making the dress ride up a bit.

"I should punish you for everything you put me through yesterday." His hand, which was on my waist, slid down to my butt.

He didn't hold back, squeezing me tightly over the fabric of the dress.

"Did I do something wrong?" I asked, apprehensive.

Our eyes were close, my hand between us. Without touching him, not knowing how to react, as if my brain were slow from the previous night and waking up suddenly in the governor's house.

"You were flaunting yourself in front of my men. Luckily, they all sign a confidentiality agreement to work with me." His hand traveled down my thigh, squeezing there. "You arrived at my place, and when I laid you on my bed, you just sprawled out and kept moaning in your sleep, hugging one of my pillows. Not to mention, you practically showed me your entire ass..."

"That's no news to you," I whispered, cutting him off.

"Now I see that the girl I know is coming back," he declared, "but that wasn't all. The things you keep saying, 'I have a fiancée,' you need to stop talking about me like that. If you keep it up in public, I'll have to reprimand you."

"A fiancée who isn't even real," I murmured, remaining still on his lap.

"Yes, but to everyone else, it's real." The hand that wore his engagement ring rose to tuck my hair behind my ear.

"Do you plan to fall in love with her after the marriage?" I asked, for the first time being invasive about his life.

"No, there will never be love between me and Keith"—he spoke with conviction about his desires.

"But... but... what about children?" In response, he just shrugged his shoulders.

"I haven't thought about that." His face was moving closer to mine slowly.

I wanted that kiss, I had waited for it my whole life, and it absolutely couldn't be under these circumstances—waking up from a tense night, hungover, and with the risk of having the worst morning breath ever.

"Did you turn your face?" he whispered in a husky voice, kissing my neck, his lips brushing my skin.

"No, you're not going to kiss me. My breath is awful, I just woke up, and I'm so thirsty, not to mention hungry," I said, closing my eyes as I felt the governor's lips giving me those delicious shivers.

"Come on, let's have breakfast, and then if nothing interrupts us, we'll finish our conversation." William lifted me with ease, setting me down on the floor.

CHAPTER TWENTY

Zoey

William had left a lavish breakfast spread, but he hadn't stayed to join me, taking a call and locking himself in his office to work.

I finished eating without knowing if he was still planning to have breakfast or if he had already eaten. I got up from the chair, biting the corner of my lip indecisively, when a movement by the kitchen made me see a woman approaching.

"Oh, hi," I said, startled.

"Hello, miss." The woman glanced at the table.

"I'm done eating." I realized she wanted to know if I was still going to eat.

Where had this woman come from? And how had I not seen her before? I didn't even know William had a staff member.

"If you'll excuse me," I just nodded and left the kitchen, which was connected to the dining room.

I stood in the center of the room, alone. A small smile appeared on my lips. It seemed that eating had stirred my curiosity; I walked over to the glass wall, looking out at the city below, and stood there for long seconds before heading to the back of the room, where there was a glass door. I pushed it open and found a small space with flowers and a wooden bench.

My curious eyes observed the flowers as I traced my fingers over them. That part of his penthouse was entirely new to me.

I sat on the bench, tilting my head back and focusing my eyes on the sky, but soon closed them, remaining there in silence, just me and my breathing.

"This place is soothing, isn't it?" William's husky voice made me open my eyes and look in his direction.

"I could easily set up my easel here and paint a picture." I smiled softly.

"Sometimes I forget that you're an artist." The governor began walking toward me.

"I know how to create a lot of art," I said, this time with explicit malice in my voice.

"I can imagine." William sat down beside me on the bench, turning his face toward mine.

"Is it time for me to leave now?" I asked with apprehension, as I didn't want to go.

"It's probably best..." his sentence trailed off.

I sighed deeply and got up from the bench.

"Fine, I'm ready to not see you for the next few days and pretend nothing is happening between us." I rolled my eyes, as it was always the same.

"What are you trying to say?" William asked as he also got up from the bench and followed me through his house.

"It's always the same thing. You want me, you touch me, give me little crumbs, and then send me away. You know what? I'm leaving, and I don't want to be your crumbs anymore," I said, turning to face him.

"You need to understand that you're my best friend's sister."

"I'm his sister, not yours! You need to understand that I'm a person too, I have feelings, and if you don't want anything with me, keep your hands well away from me," I retorted, turning to head toward the stairs to get my phone, which was there with my bag. "I'm a woman, just like any other, I'm a beautiful woman, and there are many men who don't see a problem with being Malcolm's sister."

I kept talking as I climbed the stairs, knowing he was following me. I entered the room, seeing that the bed was just as I had left it. The door closed behind me, making me jump. I turned my face and saw that William had closed it.

"We just need to maintain a boundary," the governor's voice was husky.

"What boundary?" I asked, stopping by the bed and facing him.

"Personal life and sexual life should not mix, only sex."

What he said made the spot between my legs throb, stirring my desire, the longing to know what it was like to be in the arms of the man I had always dreamed of, without considering the consequences, without knowing how it would all end.

"Only sex," I whispered as if to myself.

I wanted to assimilate and digest everything he had said.

In all likelihood, it would make me the other woman, the one to be discarded after sex, the sexual toy. Sex... reduced to just sex.

I should be happy; after all, it was what I always emphasized. But having the governor, being able to touch him, in that way, didn't make me feel any happier, it didn't make the butterflies in my stomach flutter wildly.

I blinked several times, my eyes fixed on the closed door.

No, for sure, having what I wanted in my thoughts wasn't how it should be in practice.

"Would that make me the other woman? If any information ever leaked, would I be considered the mistress?" I asked, the words leaving my mouth with a bitter taste.

"Theoretically, yes, but that will never happen. I wouldn't allow such a thing," William said, walking toward me with slow steps.

"But that's how I'd still feel." I moved away from him, not abruptly, just stepping to the side of the door.

"Don't want to, Zoey?" William turned, following my steps. "Know that I won't insist. I never insist on anything, I don't need to."

His words made me feel even more diminished to *nothing*.

"Alright," I just whispered, holding the doorknob and opening it.

Downcast, I left the room, feeling like my fairy tale was slipping through my fingers, a lifetime built on a dream fading away. I should have been more grounded, not idealizing William as my prince charming.

Nothing had happened between us, but it felt as if it had, even though we hadn't even kissed.

"Zoey." I turned, expecting him to say something useful or even ask me to stay. "Your shoes."

In his hand was my shoe, and I slightly opened my mouth. Nothing came out, but I needed to react, and I did, walking toward him, taking my shoe, and supporting myself against the wall as I put it on.

William didn't say anything more, nor did he insist that I stay. As he had said, he wasn't chasing anyone; his goals were clear, *sex*. And I knew myself well enough to continue not knowing what the governor's taste was like.

I wanted much more than the role of a mere mistress. It wasn't how I had envisioned it; it wasn't supposed to be this way.

The governor didn't ask me to stay, and I didn't insist.

CHAPTER TWENTY-ONE

William

Thirty Days Later...

"California Governor Targeted by Betrayal..."
"William Fitzgerald, member of a political family, betrayed by his fiancée..."
"Fitzgerald Replaced by Another Woman..."
Damn! I turned off my phone and threw it away. I couldn't stand my name being linked to those headlines anymore.

No matter how much Keith apologized, nothing made it stop. It was as if my name was tainted by something beyond my control. For the first time, I couldn't control it; everything was slipping through my fingers.

My political career was being tarnished by gossip sites. Keith even apologized, but nothing, absolutely nothing, made those men stop.

Of course, we broke off our engagement after what happened.

Keith was spotted in an apartment in France; there were paparazzi on the street, and she was photographed kissing another woman. Those photos spread everywhere.

There were even speculations that our engagement had been fake.

Keith, like me, was facing a media hell.

I continued doing my job, trying not to let the scandal reflect on my career, even though that was exactly what was happening.

Holding the glass of whiskey in my hand, I took the rest of the liquid to my lips. I got up from the armchair, picking up my broken phone from the floor without caring that it was shattered. This was already the second phone I had broken. Unlike the last one, at least this one showed the image, and I put it in my pocket.

I walked toward the stairs, knowing I needed a shower. After all, today was my aunt's birthday, and the party would be at her house in Sacramento, near my parents' home, and I would have to face all the Fitzgeralds giving me disapproving looks.

Not even all the craziness my cousin Zachary did before getting married compared to my situation.

I CHOSE NOT TO WEAR the jacket and stayed with just the button-up shirt tucked into my pants. The backyard of my aunt's house was all set up for the party, with elegant orange lights scattered around. The pool was covered to keep anyone from using it. There was even a dance floor.

My presence was soon noticed by my cousin Christopher, who gave me that look of someone who always thought they knew everything. Maybe it was a Fitzgerald trait, always thinking they know it all.

I let out a long sigh and headed toward him; after all, there was no way to avoid it. We had talked countless times about what happened, but nothing had changed.

Christopher, who was standing in front of the bar, picked up a glass of whiskey and extended it to me.

"Here, you need it," he said, with a hint of sarcasm in his voice.

"Am I that much of a mess?" I took the glass.

"A mess and tarnishing our family name," he retorted, resting his arm on the bar counter.

"I wish I could fix this mistake. Why didn't I get the fame Zachary got when he was left at the altar?" I grumbled, watching from a distance as my cousin held his daughter in his arms, who was wearing a pink dress.

"It's simple; even though that lunatic had a fake engagement and an even faker wedding, he didn't stay away from his bride, unlike you who was never around Keith," Christopher tried to make the obvious clear.

"Damn," I muttered, knowing deep down Chris was right.

Before marrying Savannah, Zachary was involved in a fake relationship, all to help a friend, and ended up being left at the altar by that same friend, which gained him many positive points.

My cousin put his daughter down, ran his hand along the side of his wife's face, who had a prominent belly from her pregnancy with their second daughter.

"How can Zachary be a father before us?" I complained to Christopher, who managed a forced smile, the kind he always made when he thought of his late wife.

"If it were up to me, he'd stay the first for a long time; I don't want another woman," he turned his face towards me.

"You know your life didn't stop, right?"

"What I know is that no one will be better than her," I followed his gaze, seeing the girl who appeared right behind Savannah.

I thought her name was Hazel, Zach's sister-in-law.

"Are you sure?" I teased, noticing he had been staring at the blonde for too long.

"I keep wondering how a woman can be so good at what she does and at the same time be irritating to talk to all the time," Christopher hated more than anything people who got involved in matters they weren't called for.

"I know exactly what that's like," I smiled, remembering the little whirlwind I hadn't seen in a few weeks.

"Sometimes I forget that she's Zachary's sister-in-law and keeps coming to our family parties, more time for my mom to fawn over her," he complained, taking a sip of whiskey.

"I think you're caring too much about the girl you say is so irritating," Chris rolled his eyes.

"Don't get carried away. Hazel is irritating, always giving those giggles to everyone, even helping the most defenseless of humans..."

"Something you'd do too," I cut him off, seeing him nod.

"Yes, you're right. But I chose that as a flaw in her, just like everything about that woman irritates me!"

At that moment, Zachary approached with a broad smile on his lips.

"What's with those faces like you ate something and didn't like it?" He immediately launched one of his jokes.

"Chris was sharing how much he finds your sister-in-law irritating," Zach placed his hand on our cousin's shoulder in response to what I said.

"You know that this insistence on hating her is just a part of you, right? Hazel is amazing, loves her niece, and is the best sister Savannah could have. I really don't understand you," Zachary accepted the glass Chris handed him.

"Since she said my problem was sex, I realized it wasn't anything like they paint it," he retorted.

"And by any chance, isn't it?" Zachary continued mocking.

"Go fuck yourself! I don't need sex to change my personality." I exchanged a quick glance with Zach, both of us laughing at Christopher knowing he was completely wrong.

My laughter soon faded when I spotted the small woman appearing beside her parents, wearing a burgundy dress, modest in the neckline, not even looking like the woman who had left my apartment devastated.

Damn!

"Looks like my whirlwind just arrived," I whispered, and my cousins knew Zoey's style and how she used to mark her territory with me even though we had nothing going on.

Fuck! Seeing her from a distance made me realize I missed her blatant advances.

CHAPTER TWENTY-TWO

Zoey

I opted for a medium-heeled sandal, knowing that the birthday party would be held in an open area.

Mrs. Grace Fitzgerald's birthday was supposed to be something more intimate, for close friends; my friend Scarlett's mother always invited my parents to those parties because they were friends.

I barely had time to look around when Scar came out of her house, her eyes searching for me, and she quickly made her way over. We met, her hands soon holding mine.

"This birthday party is such a drag; all they talk about is the end of William's engagement," she rolled her eyes.

"Hello, girls," Hazel, whom I hadn't seen in a few months, approached without even giving me a chance to talk about the governor.

"Oh, it's great you came," Scarlett immediately hugged Hazel, and I did the same.

Hazel was about our age, Zachary's sister-in-law, and sometimes joined us at the parties.

"Look, if I had known the untouchable president would be here, I wouldn't have bothered coming," she rolled her eyes. "I'm almost sure that soon the almighty will take his jet and go back to his palace..."

"I never really understood what's up with the president," I said, managing a half-smile.

"Whoever understands him will win a prize," Hazel crossed her arms. "What's the point of having that body, being such a hunk, if he has the humor of an eighty-year-old man who doesn't know how to enjoy anything?"

"He should take some lessons from his cousin on how to get women through a contract," I grumbled.

That night, I came with the intention of avoiding William as much as possible, just as I had been doing since I left his apartment.

"What happened? I thought you were dragging a truck for the governor; look on the bright side, now he's single," Hazel looked at me without understanding, the only one who knew what had happened was Scarlett, who loathed her cousin for what he did.

But as a good friend, she did what I asked, kept it a secret.

"Yes, single and even more of a jerk. A waiter passed by with a tray of champagne, and each of us took one. "Not that I've talked to him in the last few days."

"Has the passion ended?" Hazel gave a sly smile.

"I believe I will always drag a mountain for that man, but I don't accept being treated the way I was the last time we saw each other," I ended up confiding in Hazel about my meeting with William.

She, like Scar, disapproved of everything; every time I thought about it, being labeled as the other woman, the mistress, I wondered, what if the roles had been reversed, and I was the one caught with Keith?

I knew William's life was in chaos, and at times I thought about calling him to express my sympathy for his tragedy. But I didn't, because it would give the impression that I was pursuing him.

"Girl, if I were you, I would have smashed a house decoration over his head. What a jerk; sorry Scar, but these Fitzgeralds think they're the center of the universe, not even my brother-in-law, because he's another case. Only Savannah can put up with that," Hazel rolled her eyes.

"Sav is a sweetheart, and we know my brother fulfills all her wishes, but I know the reputation that precedes the men in this family," Scarlett mocked while talking about her own brother.

I took a small sip from my glass and, for the first time, looking around, I noticed from a distance that the governor was with his cousins near the bar, a place I wasn't going to.

We headed towards the women, approaching the Fitzgerald ladies. They were all together—Grace, Abigail, and Natalie.

"Did the gossips finish gossiping?" Grace asked as she saw us chatting in the corner.

"We needed to catch up," Hazel mocked.

"That's putting it mildly. I stopped by my mom's side, also there, rubbing her arm.

"Aren't you going to give your mother-in-law a kiss?" Abigail flashed a smile at me.

I moved away from my mother.

"A kiss, yes; now I can say ex-mother-in-law," I teased, hugging the lady who took my hand, confused.

"What happened? Did I lose my daughter-in-law?" Abigail, who always hoped something would happen between me and William, seemed worried.

"I think I'm freeing myself," I offered a weak smile.

"I need to give my son a talking-to," the lady patted my fingers. "I didn't want to lose hope; I confess I was even hopeful for the end of that engagement."

Abigail pursed her lips; after all, she had said several times that she disapproved of William's relationship with Keith, and she never went to visit his family.

"We know that nothing has changed in him." I looked around, seeing that the other women were talking, so I lowered my voice and asked, "But how is he dealing with all of this?"

"You know, in William's way of handling things, without asking for help, thinking he can deal with everything on his own." She forced a smile. "I just wish all this confusion would pass. I know my son is no saint, but he's still my son and it's clear that he's trying to do everything to get through this, and nothing is working."

"They're even talking about the engagement supposedly being fake, aren't they?" We were whispering as we spoke.

"Yes, they are, and let's face it, all the signs pointed to that. I just hope it doesn't reflect badly on his political career."

"William has always been a man who handled everything, I'm sure he'll get through this too." I gave her one of my sincere smiles.

"No more mother-in-law?" She insisted on the topic, pulling me in for another hug.

"Your son is too complicated," I declared amid the hug.

"But do you still like him?" She didn't know what had happened, and I wasn't going to go into the details.

"The governor will always be my weak spot." I pulled away from her, giving a sly wink. "Maybe I'll still tease him a bit, just a bit..."

I made a gesture with my finger, seeing the lady break into a wide smile, but clearly, it wouldn't be the same as it was.

CHAPTER TWENTY-THREE

Zoey

I entered the house while everyone was chatting animatedly; there weren't many people, which was, in a way, a good thing.

A drop of sweat was trickling down the side of my face. I was dancing with Scarlett and Hazel; it was nice to be with them. As for the plan, avoiding William and not looking in his direction was working perfectly.

I headed towards the restroom, wanting to dry my face without smudging my makeup. Distracted, I passed by the kitchen, holding the doorknob, and was startled when a large hand grabbed my shoulder and pulled me inside.

A small scream escaped from my throat as I entered the restroom, recognizing that masculine scent.

I turned around, my body pressed against the cold floor.

"What's your problem?" I said quickly, meeting those blue eyes fixed on me.

"I should be asking you that. What's going on?" he asked gruffly.

"I don't know what you're talking about," I said, widening my eyes as I held onto his shirt, trying to push him away, but his large body prevented me.

"You don't know? You've been ignoring me all night, not even looking at me..."

"And should I? Why should I look at you?" I arched an eyebrow in confusion.

"Because you're Zoey, the little tornado, always looking at me, insinuating yourself in the most unusual situations," he said, his gaze traveling down my chest, which was rising and falling rapidly.

"Do you miss my looks, Governor?" I gave a small, mischievous smile.

"I don't like not having your attention," he said, his thumb circling my shoulder where he held me.

"When you had it, you didn't value it," I whispered, focusing on his lips.

"What happened?" William began trailing his thumb down my bust, moving it slowly.

"Do you want me to refresh your memory? You didn't care at all about having me as your mistress. I keep wondering, if the situation were reversed, if I were the other woman caught with Keith, would you have stayed by my side?" I asked, gripping his shirt tighter, needing an answer from William.

"Yes, I would have, especially since I'd be so screwed that even your brother would want to kill me..."

"Of course, we have Malcolm." I rolled my eyes.

A small cry escaped my mouth when William abruptly placed his hands on my thighs and lifted me, with my legs wrapped around his waist while his body pressed mine even harder against the wall.

"So you're angry with me, then?" His face found its way to the curve of my neck.

"Very, very angry." My fingers traced the collar of his shirt.

"I didn't want you to feel that way." He bit my shoulder, lowering the strap of my dress.

"But I did, and I hated you so much for it." I closed my eyes as his mouth moved up, touching my chin.

"Zoey, I should never have spoken to you that way." I opened my eyes, meeting his. "I can't stop thinking about how your lips must taste..."

"Are you insisting on something, Governor? Looking for a second chance? Weren't you the one who said you weren't going after anything?" I whispered mischievously.

"I'm insisting on you, Zoey, wanting a second chance, and going after those lips that won't leave my mind." His face moved closer to mine.

By God, I should refuse, I should push him away, but there, nothing mattered. It was just me and him. And I had him exactly as I wanted, insisting. Maybe I should insist more, but I couldn't. I needed to know what it was like to be kissed by William Fitzgerald.

Without waiting for him to make a move, I tugged at his collar, our lips meeting in a rough, immediate motion. We quickly adjusted, our lips fitting together. An urgency grew inside me as my hand slid down the back of his neck and William's hand grasped my ponytail, gripping it tightly.

I felt his tongue touch the roof of my mouth. What started as an urgent kiss became more languid. I could feel his tongue exploring every corner of my mouth, sliding over mine, dominating our kiss.

William knew how to kiss. Heaven, his kiss was better than I had ever imagined, even more delicious than in all my dreams.

"Will..." I whimpered, unable to finish his name.

His lips trailed down my neck, leaving hot marks wherever they went.

"Say it, my little tornado, tell me you still want me," he growled, moving down my bust towards my breasts.

"Ah... Governor," I whimpered, gripping his neck tighter, craving more of those kisses.

"Tell me I'm still the only one dominating your thoughts," his voice carried that possessiveness I had always dreamed of hearing.

"William..." I couldn't say anything, my mouth seemed frozen, all that came out were desperate sighs.

"I need you to say it, my little Zoey." His face lifted, not touching my breast, but I could feel the slight protrusion of his member against my intimacy.

"Not everything in life comes easily, Governor." I gave a devilish smile.

Slowly, he lowered me to the ground, my wobbly legs searching for stability.

"I'll leave before we get caught." He raised a hand to touch my lip. "It's even sweeter and bolder than I thought."

He whispered without taking his eyes off my lip.

"Your mouth is smeared with lipstick, Governor; what will people think of you?" I bit the corner of my lip.

"And your lips are red; what will people think of you?" I dodged him, stopping in front of the mirror to see what I had said.

They were red, but his were smeared with lipstick.

"I think I'll stay here for a while, fixing my makeup," I declared, watching him turn to look at me through the mirror.

"I want your answer, Miss Beaumont; I want it by the end of the party," his tone carried that natural command of his.

Without waiting for my response, he opened the door and left. He would surely go somewhere else to fix the lipstick I had left on him.

I stood in front of the mirror for long seconds, my fingers touching my lip, still feeling his on mine, the stubble scraping my skin, the slight friction where he had left my neck red.

I hadn't expected that, nor had I desired anything more from the Governor. It had been clear he wanted nothing with me, but he had come after me in that restroom.

And men like William didn't lie to get what they wanted; I could feel the truth in his words, and for God's sake, I wanted more of that kiss, more of my Governor's hands.

CHAPTER TWENTY-FOUR

Zoey

It took me long seconds to leave the restroom, regaining my breath, fixing my makeup, until I finally mustered the courage to step out.

I walked towards the party, and luckily, everyone's distraction meant they didn't notice I had been gone for so long.

My curious eyes searched for the Governor, finding him next to a woman I didn't recognize. I furrowed my brow, trying to remember who she was.

"She's a friend of my mother's." I turned my face as I heard Scarlett's voice.

"She just arrived?" I asked, confused.

"Yes, a few minutes ago." Scar shrugged. "Did she bother you?"

"Actually, yes." I bit the corner of my lip.

"Do you want to provoke him? I caught my cousin looking at you almost all night," my friend continued with her attempts.

"I do want to, but something happened." I gave Scarlett a mischievous smile.

My friend realized what I meant, barely containing a squeal. She pulled me aside and made me recount everything, and of course, I did—the way William came after me, practically begging for the kiss.

"No way." Scarlett covered her mouth with her hand.

"Well, I could be joking, but I still feel his lips on mine."

My thoughts wandered to William's hands, the way he grabbed me, pressing me against the wall.

"But now he's with that woman..." My sentence trailed off as I looked for the Governor, wanting to know where he was.

"He might just be talking to her," Scar tried to offer some argument.

"And if he's not?" I brought the tip of my finger to my mouth, biting it.

"We can find out." My friend linked her arm with mine, pulling me along.

We walked towards the people. Hazel was dancing happily next to her three-year-old niece; it was clear how well the two got along. My friend guided me closer to where William was.

I thought she wouldn't stop right next to her, but that's exactly what she did.

"Bridget, mommy is looking for you." Scar knew the woman, indirectly sending her away.

"She is? I just spoke to her," the woman said. She was too young to be Grace's friend but old enough to be with William.

"Yes, dear." My friend gave one of her forced smiles, one I knew very well.

"We'll talk later, dear." I almost rolled my eyes when she put her hand on William's shoulder. "You know my number; if you need a shoulder to cry on, just call."

If I were Zoey from a few weeks ago, I would have shut her down, saying he didn't need that. Maybe that's what William expected me to do since he kept looking at me as if waiting for me to say something.

I held back, telling myself I wouldn't do that anymore, and I didn't.

Bridget, after realizing she didn't get any reaction from William and with a fake smile, walked away.

"I bet Aunt Grace isn't looking for her." William put his hand in his pocket, looking at his cousin.

"Do you want to continue your chat, cousin?" Scar retorted in her best confrontational manner with her cousins.

"Actually, no." William shrugged, his eyes meeting mine. "I missed your interruptions."

"It's not something that concerns me," I tried to snub him, pretending I didn't care.

"I'll be right back; I'm going to find something to drink." Scarlett, the good friend who did everything to put her plans into action, left me there.

I was left alone with the Governor, where we were, there weren't many people close by. In one of his hands, he held a glass of whiskey.

"Have you thought about what I said?" he finally asked.

"I didn't have time, and besides, you were quite busy," I spoke without holding back how jealous I was.

"For someone who doesn't find it relevant, you seem quite concerned." He gave one of his smug smiles.

"You kissed me, and minutes later, you were talking to someone else. What do you want me to think?" I crossed my arms.

"It was her who came to talk to me; I didn't call anyone." William shrugged. "In fact, I didn't even want Bridget by my side; I wanted someone else."

The Governor's eyes slid over my body, making clear what he wanted.

"Of course, there's an urgent need for some women to think they need to console the poor betrayed Governor." I rolled my eyes.

"Are you jealous, little one?" William took a step closer to me.

"Jealous of you? Never." I wrinkled my nose, trying my best to stay unaffected by his charms.

"Yes, you are." The Governor stopped very close to my body.

I looked around and noticed that we were being watched.

"They're watching us," I whispered.

"Fuck it." He seemed overtaken by something I had never seen before.

"What do you plan to do?" I asked, taking a step back.

"Actually, I wanted to kiss you in public..."

"No, I know you; you don't do that unless there's a second intention." I looked at those clear blue eyes, confused.

"Maybe there is..." William was assuming a predatory stance. "Come take a walk with me."

He motioned with his head, wanting me to follow him. At the back of Grace's property, there was a small yard with many trees where, if we went in, we could avoid being seen by many.

"They might miss us," I said, not immediately agreeing.

"They won't miss us, and if they do, they'll think you're just flirting with me and that I'm too arrogant to want anything with you." William began walking as if he knew I would follow him soon.

I let out a long sigh; it was obvious I wanted to follow him.

My heels were appropriate for this kind of place, so I had no trouble walking. The area quickly became dark, with no lighting in that part. Unsure of where I was going, I just walked straight.

"William?" I called his name.

"Are you scared, little tornado?" I could hear his voice somewhere.

"I don't like the dark much," I whispered, turning my head in all directions.

"Do you think I'd leave you alone?" I was startled to feel his lips close to my ear.

I turned, wanting to touch him, but the Governor wasn't there. I turned my face, seeing the party in the distance.

"If you don't show up now, I'll go back to the party." I stamped my foot, stopping my walk.

"Don't be afraid." I felt his hand circling my wrist, pulling me.

"What are we doing?" I gasped when the Governor's body pressed against mine from behind.

"I'm here, my little one; there's no reason to be afraid." His long fingers brushed my hair to the side.

"It's hard not to be afraid," I murmured, trying to turn but being prevented by him.

"Shhh... you don't know how much I've been thinking about your body, about how it must fit perfectly with mine," his voice was almost a whisper.

Without stopping, I knew we had entered that small yard with the trees; I could no longer hear the music clearly.

"What are you doing?" I felt my body pressed against a tree, my face against the trunk.

"Giving you what you wanted the most..."

"What I wanted the most?" I widened my eyes as his hands lifted my dress, moving over my butt. "William!"

"Shut up, damn it!" he roared. "I need you; I need to feed this need that consumes me, the desire to fuck the girl who's been messing with my thoughts..."

His voice faded as he bit my butt, a squeal escaping my mouth.

"Damn little nymphet messing with my mind, I'm going to fuck you so hard you'll never forget the man who ravaged your cunt."

That version of the Governor was entirely new to me, and I admitted it was making me extremely aroused.

CHAPTER TWENTY-FIVE

Zoey

I gripped the tree trunk tightly when I heard rustling on the ground, the noise made by William as he knelt.

"Your pants will get dirty..." My voice trailed off as I felt the Governor's face press against the middle of my ass while he bit my panties and pulled them with his teeth.

His fingers gripped the side of the fabric, tearing it with the urgency of his need.

I don't know what he did with the panties; I only felt his tongue tracing the entire length of my ass as I instinctively pushed it out.

"I need your body, little tornado..." he growled, his lips brushing against my pussy.

The tip of his tongue slid over my clit, my legs spread, and I wanted more. I was being consumed by the pleasures of my body.

William dragged his tongue over my pussy, flicking over the honey I could swear was dripping from my intimacy.

"William... ah... William." It was better than any of my dreams.

"I want to fuck your pussy," he whispered as he licked me. "Pound it hard to the bottom of this dripping little cunt."

I began to grind on his mouth, pressing my head against the tree trunk. I bit my lip hard.

"William... if you don't stop... I... I..."

"No, you're not going to come." He bit my folds to halt my movements. "I want you to squirm on my cock..."

The Governor stood up, his hand sliding to my waist, then to my shoulder, where he pushed down the sleeve of my dress and bunched it up around my stomach.

Without me turning around, I felt his body pressing against mine from behind, his large hands moving up the sides of my body, finding my breasts and squeezing them tightly.

"William..." I whimpered.

"I want to fuck you, here and now," he growled, pressing his penis against my ass.

"Yes... oh... yes..." I gasped as I heard the sound of a zipper being undone.

I rubbed my ass against his fabric. Even though I was curious to see the full extent of the Governor's penis, all I wanted at that moment was to feel his cock taking me with force.

Just pulling down his pants, I felt the Governor's protrusion press against the middle of my ass.

In a way, it wasn't how I imagined our first time, but we were talking about William, and you couldn't expect anything from him.

"I know we're outdoors, you need to stay as quiet as possible. We shouldn't be doing this, but I can't wait any longer to fuck your daring little cunt." William touched my neck, squeezing it.

"Oh... let no one see us," was all that escaped my mouth in a moan.

I rolled my eyes as he intensified his penis at my entrance, taking me as his and fucking me quickly with the first thrust, going all the way in, unable to adjust to his size, I moaned loudly.

"I'm still going to have you in my penthouse, hearing all the screams and moans this little mouth can make." With his other hand, which was squeezing my breasts, he moved up to my mouth, covering it, trying to make me quiet.

The thrusts weren't gentle; they were brutal, his member taking me with force, filling me completely as if he still needed more length to fit.

"So small... so tight," he grunted close to my ear.

My hands gripped the tree, unable to stay still, grinding on his cock.

"Fuck! That's it, grind, little one... grind that sweet ass," he roared, tightening his grip on my neck.

Even though I had had sex before, nothing compared to this; his cock was bigger, the rough and urgent way he took me drove me to delirium several times.

My small body fitting with his, the sound of our pelvises colliding against my ass, revealing that he was taking me with all his length.

He put his hand over my mouth, I brushed my tongue over it, and when William felt it, he slid two fingers inside.

"Suck my finger, give me a taste of what it would be like to have that delicious little mouth around my cock." He bit my earlobe.

To avoid letting out a cry, I ended up grinding with more urgency.

William pulled his hand from my neck and, with a slap, hit my ass. I moaned softly, running my tongue over his fingers, sucking them, as the Governor moved them in and out, as if he had his cock there.

I began to suck his fingers. The cock that was already fucking me with force started to go with more urgency, I knew it was almost there.

I tilted my head back and touched his chest. My walls clenched as I surrendered to that orgasm, and unable to hold back, I bit his fingers.

"Fuck... come, my little nymphet... come..." The Governor didn't even seem to care that I was biting him.

Surrendering, weakening, I wanted to scream but held back. With a hoarse growl, I felt his hot jets against my walls, thrusting hard one last time.

He ran his hand over my stomach and pulled my body against his. Silence took over everything again, only our heavy breathing filling the space.

I nestled into his strong chest. William removed his hand from my mouth, not even complaining about being bitten.

I remained silent as his hand moved up my breast and caressed my erect nipple.

"I want to see you naked; just feeling you like this doesn't completely satisfy me," he whispered.

"I feel the same way, Governor," I murmured, shifting to make his penis slide out of me.

William pulled up his pants, easily composed while I was still a mess. Gripping both sides of my face, his lips touching mine, he pressed my body against the tree trunk.

"I want to fuck you in my penthouse... and this time it won't be as my mistress," he growled amidst the kiss.

"What will I be, then?" I whispered, wanting to know more.

A cough near us made William quickly step away from me, aided by me pushing him.

"Where have you two been?" Scarlett complained. "For God's sake, I never want to hear my cousin and my best friend fucking again."

"Scarlett!" William reprimanded his cousin. "What are you doing here?"

"Saving your asses. Go to the party now, William. My mom said a journalist friend of hers just arrived. I don't want Zoey caught up in any sensationalist gossip." I widened my eyes.

"Damn it." The Governor cleared his throat. "I need to go..."

Even though it was dark, I felt his fingers brush against my face.

"Go on." Scar pushed him, and all I heard were his footsteps fading away. "I hope I never have to enter this darkness again; I think I've sunk my heels about three times."

"Thanks, friend," I whispered. "Thanks for saving me."

"That's what friends are for," she murmured. "You need to get ready and tell me everything. After all, I caught you in the act with my cousin. Luckily, it's dark, so I didn't have to see anything."

"I really do, sorry for the embarrassing situation..."

"It would have been embarrassing if I had seen something. I'm free from that, thank God."

I let out a weak laugh as I began to recount everything while getting ready; it felt like I could still feel all of William's fingers on my body.

CHAPTER TWENTY-SIX

William

I passed by the side of the party, not wanting to be noticed, and approached Christopher, who was alone with his glass of whiskey.

"Where have you been?" he asked as he saw me approaching.

"Just around," I replied, taking his glass from his hand.

"And I'm supposed to believe that," Chris grumbled.

He looked around, curling his lip when he saw my aunt's journalist friend, Henry Lins.

"Why does Aunt Grace keep in touch with a journalist anyway?" My cousin turned his face towards me.

"She says it's to have a journalist friend, so she can have some influence over things," Zachary answered Chris's question just then.

"Of course, and almost ruin my reputation again," I grumbled, drawing their attention.

"Where were you? I saw my sister heading towards the backyard, and now you're here, William?" Zach put his hand in his pocket.

"Well, in my defense, I didn't think your mother would invite her journalist friend," I retorted to my cousin.

"Obviously, he was somewhere with some woman," Christopher crossed his arms, giving me a hawk-like stare.

"Not just any woman," I shrugged, taking the last sip of my drink.

At that moment, Scarlett appeared with Zoey; the two of them walked with their arms linked, and I couldn't take my eyes off the little one. Even with her lips slightly reddened and an easy smile on her lips, it didn't make it obvious what we had just done.

"No way, you were with Zoey?" Zachary whispered beside me.

"Is that a problem?" I raised an eyebrow, looking at my cousin.

"Yes, hell! She's Malcolm's sister, our friend," Zach rolled his eyes. "If he finds out, he'll make sure you're castrated."

"He won't even find out..."

"You shouldn't have done that. You know the girl is in love with you. You'll play with her feelings and then discard her like you always do with every woman," Christopher tried to warn me.

"I'm not going to do that. It's just sex, and she knows that too." I looked casually at the girl walking with Scar.

It was as if I could still feel Zoey's small body in my hands, the way she surrendered, the tightness, her lips around my fingers. Now that I knew her taste, having tasted what it was like to have her, I knew I wouldn't be able to stop until I was completely satisfied.

"That's what we'll see. Just be careful; we don't want another scandal," Christopher, as always, trying to be the leader.

"Don't worry, daddy." I raised my hand to touch his shoulder.

"Our torment is approaching." I turned my face to see Henry Lins next to the insufferable Bridget.

"Is there time to escape?" I asked.

"If you do that, he'll think you're hiding something," Zachary said.

I put my hands in my pockets, standing next to Christopher, watching our torment approach.

"The three Fitzgeralds, always together," Henry started.

"Hello, Henry Lins," Christopher was the first to greet without even addressing the subject the journalist had brought up.

Next, Zachary greeted them.

"Could I have the honor of interviewing all three of you?" Lins had that smug smile on his lips.

"I don't know if you noticed, but it's my mother's birthday. We don't talk business at this kind of party," Zachary was obviously lying, as we always talked business. "Here's my assistant's number; call him."

"We both know your assistant doesn't respond to journalists." Henry gave a mocking laugh.

"He's the only one who schedules my interviews." Zachary shrugged.

Of course, the journalist's gaze fell on me.

"Besides your statement, is there nothing else?" Henry, the journalist, wanted to satisfy his curiosity.

"I have nothing more to say about it," I was rude. I wasn't used to being accommodating with journalists, and that wasn't going to change now.

"Could you give us an exclusive? After all, we all want to hear your version of the story," the journalist kept insisting.

"What I had to say, I've already said," I continued being rude.

"You Fitzgeralds are all so tight-lipped." Bridget, who had her arm linked with Henry's, said something.

We didn't say anything. We knew that in this kind of conversation, any word spoken wrong could change the context.

"Are you bothering my boys, Henry?" Aunt Grace appeared next to my mother.

"Never, dear. I'm still hoping to be favored with some exclusive." His smile was directed at me, since it was my name on all the websites.

"My son has already said everything that was necessary," Mom always defended her children.

I winked at her, smiling discreetly.

"Your son comes up with explosive news and doesn't even want us to speculate about it," Henry retorted in his best invasive journalist manner.

"Henry, Bridget, come here. I want to show you my new painting." My aunt took both of their hands, pulling them away.

My mother stayed with us for a while, waiting for them to leave before saying:

"Be careful with Henry. He's looking for any loose strand of hair. Grace only invited him to prove that our family still remains united," Mom said a bit more quietly so that only we could hear.

"I'm amazed at your perspicacity," Zachary mocked.

"We think of everything, dear." She smiled at my cousin, then turned to leave but looked back at me. "Stay away from Zoey the rest of the night. She doesn't deserve to have her photo plastered in any magazine that will slander her!"

"Yes, Mom, I won't go near her." She'd probably seen us leaving the party together, which was why she was reprimanding me so quickly.

Knowing she was right, I just nodded, and my mother walked away, leaving me with my cousins.

"I'm leaving." Christopher sighed loudly. "I've done my part as a family member, and I have a contract to review."

"Are you going back to Washington DC already?" I asked.

"No, I'll spend the night at my parents' house and leave in the morning," he said, and I nodded, understanding what he meant.

"I'll take the opportunity to leave as well. With Henry around, it's not a place I enjoy staying." I shrugged.

We had already spent too much time there, and besides, there was Capitol work waiting for me at my place, documents I brought home that I wanted to study more closely.

CHAPTER TWENTY-SEVEN

Zoey

He left without even looking in my direction. William left. Could it be because of that journalist?

"Hey, Zoey?" Scar called out to me.

"Yes?" I turned my face and realized I was a bit spaced out.

"You know Will didn't look at you or even say goodbye because of Henry," she tried to comfort me. "Henry is quite the observer. He doesn't know how our family works, and if he happened to see you giving William the cold shoulder, he might misjudge the situation. Let's just say he did it for your own good."

I nodded, knowing she was right. I still didn't understand why Grace was friends with the journalist, although I understood she wanted to maintain a perfect family image. But on her own birthday?

It was clear that William and Christopher left because of Henry's presence.

In any case, I preferred to keep my distance from the journalist. I didn't want to end up saying too much.

MY PARENTS ENDED UP leaving the party early, but since I wanted to stay longer with my friend, I stayed until the end. Scar would be staying at her parents' house, wanting to be with them, as she would soon return to campus.

I was arriving at the front of Grace's house. I was supposed to go with the Fitzgerald's driver, but what I saw there was clearly something I recognized.

"Miss Beaumont." He opened the back door. "I was instructed to take you to the governor's residence."

It was so like William. I just smiled, getting into the car and sitting in the back seat. Henry, the journalist, wasn't there anymore, so I wouldn't risk being seen.

I took out my phone as I sat down, checking the notifications, and there was one from William.

"Spend the night with me."

That was all it said. I bit the corner of my lip. It was what I wanted, to be with the governor. Although I was a bit scared about what was happening with him, knowing that all eyes were on him. What if we were caught?

"Excuse me, where are we going?" I asked the driver.

"To Mr. Fitzgerald's house," he answered promptly.

"House?" I was puzzled, as William had an apartment.

"Yes, Mr. Fitzgerald's residence." Residence?

I searched my memory, recalling that William had a house he rarely went to because he lived in the penthouse. I couldn't even remember that house anymore. Had he done this on purpose? All to avoid photographers.

THE CAR STOPPED IN front of the huge mansion, only a few lights on the first floor were on. My door was opened, and I got out of the car. I had never been here before; I only knew of its existence.

It was in a more secluded area, with a large front garden and some well-maintained rose bushes. I walked along the path of flagstones, illuminated on the sides by fixed ground lights.

I didn't even have the chance to knock on the door when it was opened by William, who immediately grabbed my wrist and pulled me inside. Aggressively, he wrapped his hands around my face, lowering his own as he closed the door with his foot.

"Damn it, I thought I'd never get out of that party," he growled, pressing his lips against mine.

"In a hurry, Governor?" His lips pressed against mine, muffling my voice.

"In a hurry to fuck this little pussy that torments me." William's tongue invaded my mouth without asking for permission, consuming me entirely.

I let him take control, feeling his tongue glide over mine like a sensual dance. His hand slid down the side of my body, moving over my legs, and effortlessly lifted me onto his lap.

"You're not wearing panties... I had forgotten that." His hand touched my ass, moving towards the center.

His finger found my opening, circling it.

"Forgot you tore my panties? Should I be worried about that?" I teased through the kiss, sliding my tongue over his lips.

I gently pulled my face away, and William started climbing the stairs with me on his lap.

"Definitely not. It's safely tucked in my pocket," he whispered, moving to my neck and leaving little bites.

My entire body shivered with his touches, as soft sighs escaped my lips.

We entered a room where he brushed his hand against a wall and turned on the light next to the bed. It wasn't bright; it was more of a dim orange. He pushed my body onto the bed and laid me down. I held his face when I realized he was about to get up; I wanted to see him up close, the man I had always dreamed of and pestered to have in my bed.

"What's wrong, little one?" he asked, raising an eyebrow slightly.

"I made it," I said with conviction. "I managed to have the governor in the same bed as me..."

A smug smile appeared on my lips.

"Have they ever told you that you're crazy?" His hands started moving up my legs.

"Almost always." I lifted my hand and unbuttoned the rest of his shirt. "The bouquet I caught at Zachary and Savannah's wedding is still waiting for you..."

William knew me so well that he knew I loved doing that kind of thing.

"I could easily marry you just to have this every day." His expression quickly turned mischievous. "How did I never see you had all this for me?"

"Because every time you saw me, you had Malcolm's image in mind..."

"Oh, I don't want to talk about that. I feel like I'm betraying my friendship with him, but I can't stay away from you anymore. It's too much temptation consuming me."

William pulled away, getting up, and I propped myself up on my elbows, watching him take off his shirt, revealing his large, defined chest, while he also unbuttoned his pants, lowering them to reveal only his black boxer briefs, which outlined his semi-erect penis.

"The briefs, Governor, give me the full package." I bit the corner of my lip, practically drooling over that man.

"Has anyone told you that you're a little slut?"

"I love being your little slut." I spread my legs, sliding one of my hands to the center of my exposed pussy, just to tease him.

William focused his attention on my movement.

"Fucking hot as hell." He took off his briefs, and his member, previously semi-erect, became increasingly hard.

His cock was huge, amazing, and made me even more excited just seeing that big man all for me.

CHAPTER TWENTY-EIGHT

Zoey

I leaned my body on my knees, moving toward the governor, who was completely naked. I ran my hand over his shoulder as I felt him lift my dress, pulling it over my head and leaving me as naked as he was.

I brought my face close to his chest, planting slow, wet kisses interspersed with small licks.

Lowering further and further, until I reached the tip of his member, seeing it up close, glorious, touching the tip of his stomach.

William grabbed the base of his cock, directing it toward me and rubbing it against my cheek.

"Do you like sucking my little slut?" he asked as a smile spread across my lips, feeling the head of his cock outline my lip.

"If it's your cock, I love it," I teased. If he knew how to provoke, I did too.

"Then suck the head of my cock." I stuck out my tongue, licking the shiny part, keeping my eyes locked on his as I took his penis into my mouth.

William briefly closed his eyes, then opened them, meeting mine. His hand moved to the back of my neck, pulling my hair into a ponytail.

"Oh, governor, if you only knew how much I've dreamed of this moment," I whispered to tease him. "Sometimes, I would wake up wet from an erotic dream with you taking me with lust..."

"Damn, little nymph..." His deep voice made me open my mouth wider as he thrust forcefully inside.

I gagged, holding tightly to his waist, but William didn't stop. With his hand in my hair, he brought my mouth back to the base of his cock. His controlling eyes were on me the entire time, tears welling up in my eyes.

I grabbed the base of his cock and took control of the situation, starting to suck him with lust, even though I was gagging. His hand still held my hair, pushing me to go deeper, but I didn't stop.

"Fucking tasty little mouth," he growled, saliva escaping from the sides of my mouth as his cock circled my lips.

I released my grip on his cock and moved to his balls, which I gently squeezed, while with my other hand, I did something I had wanted to do for a long time—I felt his ass with my fingers. I took his member out of my mouth, flashing a mischievous smile.

"Let me be your little slut," I whispered, knowing how to push a man like William to his limits; they liked everything, but outside the bedroom, they wanted to be discreet.

"Oh, my little slut." Holding my hair with both hands, William pushed my body back.

I lay down on the bed, watching him come over me. His cock stopped at my mouth again, and William held onto the headboard, thrusting quickly into my mouth, fucking me that way.

In that position, it was as if his cock touched the back of my throat more easily, the echoes of my saliva making noise. William groaned and grunted loudly.

"Damn, I'm going to come," he roared as, with one of his thrusts, I felt his hot liquid in my mouth, part of it made me swallow while the rest spurted onto my face, staying on his knees on each side of my shoulder, holding the base of his member.

He rubbed his cock on my lip, letting the last drop of his come fall there. I licked around my lips, savoring the moment.

William seemed fascinated, not taking his eyes off me for a moment.

"How can you be so..." he murmured, bringing his lips close to mine. "How can you be so slutty between four walls?"

"I couldn't be an immaculate virgin when I had my first time with you, so I tested, studied, and became a sex-crazy woman." I spread my legs as the governor positioned himself between them.

"I don't know if I like the sex-crazy part, knowing that I'm not your first man..." I ran my hand over his shoulder, touching his neck.

"Don't worry, Governor, I just had a few men to gain experience, then I used toys..." I bit the corner of my lip. "I confess, it wasn't just for you; I love having sex."

I pushed him to the side, straddling his lap.

"So, does that mean my friend's little sister is a slut?" he whispered, raising his hand and pinching my nipple.

"Your slut." I rubbed my pussy against his cock.

"As long as you're only mine..." He raised his face, licking my nipple, then taking my breasts into his mouth.

"Yours..." My head tilted back. "Only yours..."

Rolling, I guided his now erect cock into a new round, feeling him take me completely.

William sat on the bed, squeezing my ass while sucking on my breasts with force, and I started grinding faster. My hair, damp with sweat, stuck to my back.

"Damn! You're perfect, Zoey," he grunted as our eyes met. "My cum on your face just proves how much you're my little slut..."

I rolled my eyes, biting the corner of my lip. Everything was so much better than any dream I had ever had. Sensing that I was almost giving in, William held my waist, laid me on the bed, and lifted my legs, placing them together on one of his shoulders as he drove his cock into me and started fucking me hard.

He didn't know the word gentle; he always fucked me hard, with all his length.

I tilted my head back, moaning loudly.

"That's it, moan, scream, sigh, give me everything you've got, my little nymph," he grunted, not stopping his thrusts. I raised my hand to touch my breasts, squeezing my nipples, while my eyes met his, seeing the pleasure shine in those blue eyes.

"You want everything from me, governor?" I whispered lustfully, squeezing my breasts.

"I already have it." With possessiveness, he focused on my hand squeezing my breasts.

That look, where pleasure coursed through every part of my skin, made me give myself to him. Restlessly, I surrendered, tightening my walls around his cock.

I let out a little scream on that rollercoaster I was on and fell into freefall in that orgasm. It wasn't long after a few strong thrusts that William went deep, cumming forcefully, coating me with his ejaculate.

Our bodies were sweaty, exhaustion beginning to take over me.

He pulled his cock out of my pussy and moved my legs onto the bed. As our eyes met, he ran his hand beside my ear and brushed the hair from my face.

"Tired?" William whispered.

"I think so." A lazy smile spread across my lips.

"Want to take a shower?"

"I think I need to." Slowly, I started sitting up on the bed.

"Come on." He got up, stretching on the bed and lifting me onto his lap.

"What are you going to do?" I widened my eyes, not expecting that.

"Well, take a shower." He gave a confused look, as if it were nothing unusual.

"Together?"

"Yeah, I don't usually do that after sex, but I want to wash your body." He lowered his gaze, directing those intense blue eyes at me.

"So you don't shower with your hookups?"

"No, you'll be my exception." He winked mischievously. "Another one of my exceptions; it seems like everything about you is my exception."

The way he spoke seemed to be something only about him, as if he were thinking aloud and somehow, making me feel warm inside, with those silly butterflies fluttering in my stomach.

CHAPTER TWENTY-NINE

William

The water fell over Zoey's back, her black hair wet and cascading over her skin. I approached her, sliding my hand over her shoulder and down her skin.

The little one tilted her head back, resting it against my chest, making the water cascade over her breasts, leaving her nipples hardened.

Damn! If Malcolm knew I was with his sister, he'd kill me. It was becoming impossible to stay away from her, away from those always challenging looks.

It was as if a part of me had grown accustomed to it, and when it was lost, it realized how much it was missed.

With Zoey, everything was new: the first time I'd brought a woman to this house, the first time I'd showered with someone.

"William," the little one whispered, turning around and running her hand over my neck, standing on her tiptoes.

"Yes?" I asked, sliding my hand under her ass and lifting her onto my lap.

We had both already showered, and throughout the entire shower, my cock hadn't softened for a second, as if begging for that little pussy.

"Aren't we at risk of being caught here?" she asked, making a face as her back pressed against the cold wall.

"No, this is a gated community, and only my friends come here." I shrugged, pressing my cock against her little pussy.

"William..." She whimpered, biting the corner of her full lip.

"You're so tight, little one, delicious," I whispered, nibbling her earlobe, sliding in and out slowly.

This time, I made the sex slow, deliberate, savoring every inch of the little one.

Zoey's nails dragged along my back as I brought my lips to hers, fitting them in a soft, wet kiss.

At 38 years old, this was the first time I was having sex in the bathroom, but they say there's a first time for everything.

Once again, the little tornado was the first in something.

Between our kisses, Zoey moaned, scratched my back, and held me, making me completely hers.

I noticed her moans intensified the moment I squeezed her thigh with a bit more force and thrust deep with aggression. Our bodies collided and echoed in the bathroom.

I deepened the kiss, sucked on her tongue, and roared in the midst of another round of orgasms, damn!

Zoey surrendered as well; I held her body close to mine and felt her chest rise and fall rapidly against mine.

I didn't even think to ask about contraceptive methods; I always used condoms, even though they all said they were on the pill. I didn't trust enough to have unprotected sex, but with Zoey, it was different. I knew the family she came from; she'd never pull a pregnancy trap on me. I didn't worry about asking since she hadn't brought it up.

Slowly, Zoey put her feet on the ground. I helped her, we cleaned up under the shower, and I was the first to get out, wrapping myself in a towel and then grabbing another one for her.

I wrapped it carefully around her, keeping her warm.

"You seem like a romantic man," she teased mischievously, grabbing another towel to dry her hair.

"When there's something I want, I can be," I mocked, leaving the suite and entering the closet where my clothes were. However, since I didn't stay there much, I didn't have many clothes in the house.

I put on a pair of underwear and then sweatpants. I turned to see the little one entering the closet.

"Do you have a shirt I could borrow?" she asked, biting the corner of her lip mischievously.

I nodded, grabbing one of my running shirts and handing it to her. Zoey took off the towel wrapped around her body, wearing just the shirt. The fabric fell slightly above her knee, the nipples of her breasts pressing against the shirt's fabric.

She was absolutely perfect.

Her long, damp hair fell in cascades around her shoulders, her dark eyes meeting mine as she caught me staring at her.

"Lost something, governor?" Without waiting for my response, she turned and walked towards the bedroom.

I just shook my head as I watched her go to the other side of the bed.

"What's the story with this house? Why do you have it?" she asked curiously.

"I like it, it's large, has a vast backyard, and a library downstairs, an ideal place to raise a family." I shrugged casually.

"It just lacks the essential thing, a family." Zoey gave me one of her charming smiles.

"One day I'll have one, and I'll have the house too..."

"And what if your wife doesn't like it?" she asked as I lowered the blanket, our eyes meeting.

"I don't know, wouldn't you like it?" I asked, forgetting that this woman had once been in love with me.

Zoey looked around, sat on the bed, tucked her feet under the blanket, and I did the same, waiting for her response.

"I didn't see much of the house, but I can imagine miniatures of Fitzgerald shouting through these corridors." I dimmed the light, making the room darker. "But if I were your wife, I'd hate to know my husband was bringing women into the house where we have our family."

Zoey tucked her hair behind her ear, her eyes locked on mine.

"You're the first I've brought here. I've always thought I'd only bring my chosen one to our home." I moved closer, lying her down on the bed, my body covering hers, stroking the side of her face with my fingers.

"I know this isn't a marriage proposal." Zoey smiled.

"Definitely not. I needed you, I could have taken you to a hotel, but I didn't want to risk being spotted by someone else, so I brought you to my safest place." I brought my lips close to hers, giving her a lingering kiss.

"And in return, you're showing me the place where you plan to start your family." She rolled her eyes playfully.

"Why? I mean, why this fixation?" I asked, confused.

"Why not you? Christopher got married young, he's too serious, and when he was married, it was clear he only had eyes for his wife, and they met in college. Zachary, I don't know, maybe because he's Scar's best friend, I ended up seeing too many flaws in him." She let out a soft laugh.

"I guess I'm more flawed than my cousin..."

"But you caught my attention from the first moment I saw you, and I was just a kid dreaming of a prince charming."

"What changed?"

"The prince turned into a frog," she teased, pushing my chest. "I'm tired, can we spoon?"

"Your wish is my command..."

It was easy being with Zoey; she might be a little tornado, but with all the chaos she exuded, there was also a charming woman who liked to talk. I could easily adapt to her fiery way of living.

CHAPTER THIRTY

Zoey

His arm around my waist tightened as if I could escape, waking me up. I opened my eyes to the room lit by daylight.

I ran my fingers over his hand, remembering who he was, my governor. His fingers were long, covering the entire length of my stomach. The sigh William gave revealed that he was waking up.

His fingers gripping the fabric of the shirt I was wearing.

"Good morning, governor," I whispered with a lazy voice.

"Hello, little one," he murmured, removing his hand from my stomach and placing it in my hair, pushing it away from my face.

I turned on the bed and lay on my back, my face towards his. William had slightly messy hair. His eyes were a blue like a cloudless sky.

"Did you sleep well?" he asked, sliding his finger along the side of my face.

"After all the exercise we had last night, there was no way not to sleep well." I gave a lazy smile.

"Are you hungry?" he asked, leaning over my body, covering me with his.

"Starving." William moved off me, standing up.

"Wait a moment, I asked them to bring something for you." He turned, opened the door as if grabbing something from outside, and came back with a bag from a brand I loved. "I asked them to buy clothes for you. I don't want you going out in my shirt or that dress from yesterday without underwear."

He pouted and placed the bag in front of me. I opened it and looked inside. I pulled out a lingerie set from a small envelope and, removing the paper, revealed a black lace piece.

"Who buys these clothes?" I asked suspiciously.

"There's a store where I have an account; I just call and ask for the size I want, sometimes I choose the styles." He sat on the bed, watching me.

"Do you do this with all the women you date?" I asked curiously.

"Yeah, in some cases, yes." He frowned.

"I'm not sure if I'm too thrilled about that." I picked up the dress from the bag, unfolded it, and noticed the nude color that matched my skin tone.

"These are tactics I've developed to make things more practical, so women leave more quickly the next day." He shrugged casually.

"Was that a hint? Do you want me to leave?" I widened my eyes.

"Of course not, I want to have breakfast with you." He winked.

I set the bag aside, threw off the blanket, and got up, letting out a squeal as William grabbed my wrist and pulled me closer to him. I lost my balance and grabbed his shoulder.

"William!" I gasped, sitting between his legs.

"Little one." My eyes fixed on his large hand on my bare thigh, my skin tingling at his touch. "You're beautiful, even with your crazy ways, you're a genius and amazing girl. But..., but..."

"We don't need to talk about this." William cleared his throat and I continued. "We don't need to label anything. I know you're my brother's best friend, and I'm just the crazy girl who's always been in love with the governor. That's how our families will always see it, and let them think that way."

I shrugged, trying to show that I didn't care, even though I did. It was all I wanted. To live beside that man who had my heart. At first, it might have been just a crush from a deluded girl, but getting to know the governor better made my silly heart beat faster.

"So you don't care?" He raised an eyebrow slightly.

"No." I bit the corner of my lip, running my hand over his neck.

"Not even with your comments about marrying me?"

"Totally over it." I gave my best fake smile.

"I really value my friendship with Malcolm, I don't want what we had to ruin that friendship."

He spoke as if it were in the past, making me understand that our sex would not happen again.

"I wish this situation were different, that you weren't my best friend's sister, that you were at least ten years older." He let out a loud sigh.

"Would that change anything?" I asked.

"Actually, yes, it would be easier to be involved with an older woman. What would my voters think if I showed up with a 19-year-old?" He gave one of his typical forced smiles, the kind that seemed to want to come to terms with something.

"Zachary didn't mind marrying Savannah, and she's younger than him," I said, finding a pretext.

"Zachary had no choice; she showed up pregnant..."

"We know it wasn't exactly like that. Your cousin is crazy in love with Sav; he wasn't forced into anything; he wanted it," I cut in quickly. William was clearly on the defensive.

"Yes, you're right; that's not our case." I simply nodded, getting up from his lap.

"I just don't want your regret or pity, please." I stretched my arms, grabbing the change of clothes.

"Are you mad at me?" He grabbed my wrist, making me look at him again.

"Never, William. You simply could have spared this pleasant morning with this unpleasant conversation," I said bluntly.

"I needed you to understand that there's no possibility of us getting married, even if I wanted to. It's far from everything I've planned for my life, even going against my political position." William wanted to spare me from potential emotional pain.

"I'm marvelously fine." I gently pulled my arm away, wanting to go to the bathroom.

"Little one..."

"You should have thought about all this suffering before bringing me to your house, where you plan to build your family, your wife, giving me a free sample of what it's like to be with a man like you." I rolled my eyes, wanting at least to be alone in the suite.

"Yes, the mistake was entirely mine," was all he said.

It wasn't his fault; it was mine. I wasn't forced to come here; I wanted to. I needed to know what it was like to be with the man I had always dreamed of being with. He was perfect, intense, far better than any dream.

I was a woman; I needed to face all the consequences of my actions, and that's what I was doing. I knew that William would never accept me as his, given the numerous factors that divided us.

CHAPTER THIRTY-ONE

Zoey

The clothes he had sent for me, like the other ones, fit perfectly. I stood in front of the bathroom mirror, tying just part of my hair into a messy bun, leaving the rest loose around my neck, where I noticed a purple mark. I moved closer to the mirror to see more clearly the hickey William had left there.

We were so eager for each other that I hadn't even noticed he had done that.

I turned around and opened the suite door, finding that the governor was no longer in the room. He had probably gone downstairs. I spotted my bag next to the bed and went to grab it.

After our brief argument, I believed it was best to leave. I looked around; the bed was still messy, knowing that this would remain just a distant dream. It was clear that there were millions of reasons separating us, and William would not bother to face them.

Perhaps, when it came to me, I wasn't worth the effort for him.

I left the room and heard William's voice on the first floor. Was he talking to someone on the phone? I didn't even bother to listen to what he was saying; I just headed for the stairs and began descending them. During the day, the house seemed even brighter and bigger.

My bare feet touched the first steps, slowly descending one by one. From the stairs, I had a view of the entire living room, where I turned my face, widening my eyes when I saw who was there—my brother.

"Zozo, what are you doing here?" Only he and Scar still called me that.

I parted my lips, unsure of what to say. How hadn't William told me Malcolm was here? Not knowing what to say, I looked for help from William.

But my look was clearly a warning signal to Malcolm, who turned his gaze towards William.

"What the hell is my sister doing in your house?" Malcolm took a step towards the governor.

"Malcolm..." William tried to speak, but my brother had already taken in everything.

"Damn it, William!!! She's my sister, for fuck's sake," he roared, going after the governor, shoving him in the chest, catching William off guard and making him fall onto the sofa.

Everything happened so fast that by the time I saw it, Malcolm had already knelt on the sofa and, with his fists clenched, threw a punch to the side of the governor's face.

"MALCOLM!" I yelled, running down the stairs towards my brother.

Even after taking a punch, William grabbed my brother by the collar, trying to push him away, which was obviously difficult given his disadvantageous position.

"Let me explain, damn it!" William roared, but Malcolm was clearly blinded by rage, throwing another punch to the same spot on the governor's face.

"MALCOLM" I yelled again, grabbing his jacket, trying to pull him back. "LET HIM GO, FOR GOD'S SAKE! LET GO!"

I screamed in desperation. It seemed that my plea made my brother momentarily distracted, allowing William to push his face forward, hitting Malcolm's mouth, making him step back.

William got up but didn't go after my brother; he kept a good distance.

Malcolm wanted to go back at William, but I positioned myself in front of him, holding onto his shirt with all my strength to prevent another physical confrontation.

"Bastard, damn it!" My brother put his hand to his lip, where a small drop of blood glistened.

"Enough, Malcolm!" I pleaded, my eyes meeting his.

"Enough, is it?" My brother growled, looking over my shoulder and narrowing his eyes. "I'm going to kill you, you bastard! I asked countless times not to lay a finger on Zoey. You knew better than anyone that I didn't want my best friend involved with my little sister, you scoundrel..."

"Brother! Enough! I'm not a child anymore; I know very well my actions and their consequences," I said, stamping my foot on the ground, overwhelmed with despair, and I hadn't even realized that tears of fear were streaming down my face.

"No, Zoey, the problem here is between me and this bastard. He owes me his loyalty. He promised never to touch you, knowing that you had this damn crush on him." I turned my face, seeing that William had his hand by his face, which was clearly red.

"Brother..."

"No, I'm not your brother," Malcolm roared at William, not letting him speak. "I know your background; I know you're not capable of committing to anything serious. All I asked was that you keep your hands off Zoey, and it seems even that is too much for you..."

"Damn it!" William cursed. "It happened, alright? Maybe you should take that blindfold off your eyes; she's not a little girl anymore."

"Yeah, what would you say if I fucked Scarlett, huh?" I widened my eyes at how Malcolm spoke.

"My cousin would never sleep with you!" William growled.

Both were furious.

"Enough, for the love of God, enough!" I begged, fearing another physical confrontation.

A silence fell over the room. I felt Malcolm's body relax, realizing that he would calm down.

"Tell me, William, do you have any intentions with my sister?" he asked, directing his gaze at the governor.

Again, silence filled the room. I turned my face, looking at William's expression, remembering the conversation we had, where he said he would never be with me.

"That's what I expected," Malcolm mocked.

"You know I'm not having the best time of my life," William argued.

"And that's why you decided to take my sister to bed? What selfishness on your part." Malcolm let out a forced laugh.

"William, is that your final answer?" This time, it was me who asked, feeling the tears streaming down my face.

"We talked about this; you knew from the beginning..."

"It's better this way; you don't deserve my sister; she's too good for a scoundrel like you," Malcolm interrupted again. "I want you to stay away from Zoey. If I find out about anything, I'll smash your face, got it?"

At that moment, I saw their friendship breaking apart.

"Malcolm, you know I would take her without any difficulty," the way the governor spoke was like reigniting a small flame within me.

"No! Stay away from Zoey, far away," Malcolm didn't even argue, making it clear that he would never approve of our relationship.

William did not insist, and everything became clear; he would not face our difficulties for me. The small flame that had ignited inside me quickly extinguished.

"Please, brother, take me home," I pleaded, wiping under my eyes.

I couldn't hide my sadness, all my disappointment, and in part, it was my fault. William had never promised me anything, but being rejected by him again, as always, hurt more than before, especially since I now knew what it was like to be with him, in his arms.

CHAPTER THIRTY-TWO

William

I released the tension I hadn't realized I was holding in my shoulders. My face throbbed with the persistent pain from the two punches I had taken.

Damn it! It wasn't supposed to end like this. I circled around the sofa and sat down on it, running my hand over my face. What the hell was Malcolm doing here?

When the doorbell rang, I thought it could be anyone but him.

I didn't even get the chance to tell Zoey not to come downstairs, to stay hidden in my room.

From what I understood, Malcolm wanted to discuss a contract we were going to sign. He was always very hasty; when he decided on something, he wanted it done yesterday. And clearly, he must have found some free time in his schedule and came to California to settle it.

What I didn't expect was for it to be now, and on that particular day.

Malcolm arrived saying he had stopped by my apartment and, not finding me there, called my assistant to ask where I was, and of course, my assistant told him.

That house wasn't a secret to those close to me. When I saw it, it was love at first sight, and even though I didn't have a wife, I knew it was where I wanted to build a family. Although after that day, it would be marked in my mind, not in a very good way.

The wonderful night I had with Zoey ended in the worst possible way. Her expression, the explicit sadness, the tears streaming down her face, etched in my mind, I had hurt her, hurt the girl who had always made it clear that she had always loved me.

If that didn't make me a monster, I didn't know what could.

I was frozen in every sense. Zoey expected me to take some action, to run after her, but my feet were immobilized. Everything I was feeling at that moment left me confused; I had never wanted to be with someone as much as I wanted to be with her.

I could have been less selfish if I hadn't hesitated at first, but I hesitated, and Malcolm noticed. When he said I wasn't good enough for his sister, he had already noticed that there was no absolute certainty in my words.

Deep down, he was right; I was too much of a scoundrel to deserve such a sweet and charming woman like Zoey.

Even when I convinced myself that she was just my friend's sister, there was some moment I can't pinpoint when that little whirlwind touched something inside me. She had me, truly had me.

But there were countless reasons that separated us. Her age, what my voters would think of me being with a woman who could even be considered a daughter. If only Zoey were ten years older, it wouldn't be a problem, but the nineteen-year age gap between us was glaring, and she was there, shouting loudly as one of the many things that divided us.

Not to mention now the part where her brother hated me.

I got up from the sofa, knowing I needed to put a compress on my face, or else my eye would be even more bruised.

I should have been stronger, more resilient, but I wasn't. I let myself be carried away, but I didn't regret it. I was with that little one; it wasn't just a dream, it wasn't a fantasy.

The hell of it was that now everything on my mind was Zoey Beaumont.

The way she smiled, the way she curled her lips when something displeased her, the bite on the corner of her lip when she wanted to tease, her dark eyes with those lashes that highlighted her beauty when she blinked, her long, wavy dark brown hair.

It was much easier when Zoey was just Malcolm's sister, the crazy girl who told everyone she was my future wife. But now she had become so much more than that, being the woman who dominated my thoughts.

The small tornado that had always been there, which gained strength when it came in and devastated my entire life.

I couldn't let myself be carried away by those feelings; I needed to be strong, for my career as governor, for the image I had always maintained knowing that with her came all my family's connections.

Fitzgerald had always been synonymous with a discreet and educated family; I wouldn't be the one to tarnish our name.

If rejecting Zoey was the most painful thing I needed to do in my life, then let it be done with my head held high, even though that pain consumed me from within, squeezing my chest like never before. Why the hell did I give the key to my heart to that little one? Because I was weak and not resilient, now I had screwed up everything, absolutely everything.

I STOOD IN FRONT OF the mirror, five days after the beautiful punch Malcolm had given me; the bruise was still present in my eyes.

My mother continued to hate me for what I had done to Zoey. It seemed that my entire family hated me, as no one bothered to send even a single message asking how I was.

Except for my cousins, who had stayed by my side, offering their advice. There was no chance of anyone being on my side. After all, even I knew I shouldn't have done what I did to Zoey.

Every time I tried to call her, it went to voicemail, and the messages I sent weren't even received.

It all pointed to me being blocked. I just wanted to apologize, to know how she was, I cared about her. And damn it! I missed that little fiery one.

But everything was against me.

I adjusted my tie, grabbed my sunglasses; it would be another day where I hid my eyes behind them.

Fortunately, or unfortunately, my involvement with Zoey remained within the family; no journalist found out. Not that it was wonderful, since it spread throughout my family, as Zoey's mother was friends with mine. And from what I heard, her father wanted my hide.

It was great. Lately, I went from the Capitol to my apartment and back, after all, I was the 38-year-old man who ended up with my best friend's little sister. I was being hated by everyone.

And the worst part of all was that I deserved it, I deserved all of it.

CHAPTER THIRTY-THREE

Zoey

I threw the brush beside the workbench, irritation taking over me once again.

All of this, all the people surrounding me, asking if I was okay as if I were a crystal about to shatter. I couldn't even paint; everything was about the man who wouldn't leave my mind, William.

If I had known it would be such a hell, I would have thought twice...

Who was I kidding? It was obvious I wouldn't think twice; I would do everything again.

I might be living through chaos in my life, but I could say that I had what I always wanted, William Fitzgerald, even if it wasn't entirely, even if it was just for one night, and now only the memories of a wild night remained.

"Dear?" A knock on my door made me turn my face, seeing my mother smiling.

"Hi, Mom." I got up from my stool.

"No inspiration?" She gave one of her forced smiles.

"More or less." I took a cloth, drying the paint that had stained my fingers.

"You know, if I could, I would do everything to make sure none of this happened."

"Mom, let's look on the bright side, it didn't make it to the media." I left the cloth beside me and headed toward the door.

"Your brother is going back to Springfield; do you want to say goodbye?" Malcolm had spent five days here, helping my father with family gallery matters.

"Yes." I smiled, following her down the hallway to the living room, where I found my father and brother.

When Malcolm talked about the incident with my parents, I thought I could bury my face in a hole and disappear at that moment. My father wanted to kill William, and Mom's eyes widened so much I thought they might pop out.

I hadn't expected that this story would spread to the Fitzgerald household and that they would all end up knowing.

It was so quick that Scar heard about it from someone else before hearing it from me.

I entered the room, and my brother got up from the sofa. I didn't want Malcolm and William's friendship to end like this, because of me.

"Zozo, how are you feeling?" he asked with his usual concerned tone.

"I'm fine, just like yesterday and how I'll be tomorrow." I shrugged my shoulders.

"Have you thought about the proposal I made you?" he asked.

"Yes." Apprehensively, I bit the corner of my lip and looked at my mother.

"Dear, go spend some time in Springfield with your brother; I'm sure that being away from here for a bit will do you good." Mom winked. "Not that I want you to be away, but I want the best for you."

"Thank you, Mom," I said, knowing I had a great family that supported me in everything.

"So, what do you say? Grandpa will love having your company." My brother lived in the same house as our maternal grandfather.

Ralph was a lively old man, sometimes a bit grumpy, but he did everything for his only grandchild.

"Only if you promise me you won't bar my friend Scar from entering just because she's a Fitzgerald." Malcolm grimaced when I mentioned the surname.

"I don't want to hear that surname anytime soon, but I won't forbid her entry; after all, the girl isn't to blame for her cousin..."

"Please, let's not talk about it," I cut him off, as he obviously didn't want to mention the governor.

"Okay, okay..." he simply nodded, realizing it was a sensitive topic for me.

"Mom, I don't want to stop my studies; if you manage to speak with Mrs. Joss, tell her that I will continue doing all the activities remotely," I said, seeing my mother nod.

"I'll make sure to tell her."

"I'll just pack my bags, and then we can leave."

I turned and left the room. Malcolm had made that offer on the first day I left William's house, knowing it could be difficult for me. In their minds, once again, the governor had been a jerk to me.

In truth, I couldn't really blame William for everything, but deep down, very deep down, there was a growing anger. He said nothing that day, letting my brother take me away.

It was clear that William would always let our differences speak louder.

MY BROTHER'S JET LANDED in the back area of Mr. Ralph Ross's mansion. Malcolm's mother came from a billionaire family, and as an only child, she inherited everything. Now it belonged to my brother, the only child she ever had.

Mr. Ross always got along well with my father, and my brother often said that his grandfather used to tell my dad that he needed to move on because it wasn't what his daughter would want.

Malcolm seemed to have been born with the political gene inherited from his grandfather, who had also been the governor of Illinois.

Through the window, I saw the jet doors open, and I slowly unfastened my seatbelt. I felt it would be good to spend that time with my brother.

It would be nice to be a little away from William and all the concern his family had about me.

"Shall we?" Malcolm extended his hand to me.

He was tall, with hair as black as mine, kept trimmed on the sides and a bit longer on top.

"Yes." I smiled, taking his hand.

I got up from the seat and walked in front of him. A gentle breeze touched my arm as I reached the stairs. I looked around; it had been a while since I had been here.

It was amazing how Malcolm lived in an even more luxurious reality than mine. The mansion was enormous, with a covered pool in one corner, and even a flower greenhouse. I kept wondering if they ever used all the amenities of that house.

I descended one step at a time, letting out a long sigh, hoping that here, away from my governor, I could manage to forget him, which I knew probably wouldn't happen since I hadn't forgotten him in my teenage years. What were the chances now!

I needed to be strong and remind myself of all the times William had rejected me, and none of those times had he made a great effort to come after me.

CHAPTER THIRTY-FOUR

Zoey

30 Days Later...

"Friend, if you don't go, I'm going out to buy it." Scar sat on the bed in the room where I was sleeping.

"This has to be madness, what's the chance of getting pregnant?" I tossed my hair back.

"All of them? They fucked like rabbits and thought what? If you're in the rain, you're going to get wet, my friend..."

"But I took that damn morning-after pill," I murmured anxiously.

"Two days later, you know the pill is for the morning after, not two days after." Scarlett was insisting that I take a pharmacy test.

"You're right," I whispered, biting the corner of my lip, nervous.

"Want to go out to buy it?" she asked, getting up from the bed.

"Yes, let's go now."

I grabbed my handbag from beside the bed.

"Do you think Mr. Ralph would lend us one of his cars?" My friend flashed a small smile.

"You've become quite friendly with my brother's grandfather." I frowned.

Scarlett had come to spend a week with me; we had missed each other, and with all that drama that happened, we hadn't had time to meet up.

"Ralph is a good man..."

"You know he usually isn't, right?"

"I always see him being nice to you." She frowned in confusion.

"That's because I'm considered part of his family; he doesn't usually open up to outsiders. He liked you." I shrugged as I left the room with her.

"Well..." Scar repeated my gesture and shrugged.

We descended the steps of the enormous house; I didn't know how my brother and Mr. Ralph didn't get lost inside. I reached the last step and looked to the side where my brother's grandfather was.

"You're going out, dears?" he asked with a sideways smile. It was strange to see him smile since he was always serious.

"Yes, do you know if my brother has already left?" Malcolm had come for lunch; he didn't come often, but since I arrived, he had been coming more frequently, or so Ralph said.

"I'm here." I raised my face to see him adjusting his tie.

"We're going out. Scar needs to buy one of her medicines that's run out." I tossed the ball to her, and she didn't mind, since my brother knew I only took vitamins, and they were all up to date.

"Do you want a ride?" he asked helpfully.

"Actually, we wanted to see if Mr. Ralph would lend us one of his cars," Scar said, looking at Malcolm's grandfather.

"I doubt it," my brother whispered, and we all looked at Mr. Ralph, waiting for his response.

"Promise to take good care of it?"

"Like it's a baby," Scar answered promptly with a broad smile.

"The keys to all my cars are in the rack next to the garage," Ralph authorized, and Scar gave a squeal of happiness as she went to him, bending down to his wheelchair and giving him a kiss on his cheek.

"Are you serious? You're really lending us a car?" My brother seemed stunned beside me.

"Yes." The man winked at Scarlett. "Especially with a smile like that on her face."

It was clear he spoke with affection, as if treating her like a family member. Even as if she were the daughter he lost.

"You're so sweet." She returned the gesture, winking back at him.

Scar and Ralph even played chess together; my friend also played the piano that once belonged to my brother's mother. Scarlett was a great pianist, and it seemed she had won Mr. Ralph's heart.

"Let's go, friend." Scar made a motion with her hand for me to follow.

I said goodbye to Malcolm with a hug, then did the same with the man who had always been very kind to me.

Living there was like living on permanent vacation; I had everything I wanted on demand, many servants in the halls, and always someone at my disposal, with the one exception—my online classes.

"What about you and Mr. Ralph?" I asked when we were alone in the garage.

"Nothing, why?" she retorted, looking at all the cars parked there.

To me, they were just old cars, but to my friend, they seemed like precious jewels.

"The way he treats you is different." Scar looked at the number of one of the car's parking spots.

"It's all in your head; we just get along really well..."

"And what about my brother?" She stopped, looking at me.

"What about him?" I furrowed my brow further.

"I don't know, you both are acting strange, like you've talked about something without me knowing. — I crossed my arms.

"We haven't talked; I'd tell you if something like that happened. He's pretty hot, no denying that, and well, I... I... was caught in the act." Scar's cheeks turned bright red.

"Oh God! Scarlett, what happened?"

"Last night, I woke up in the middle of the night thirsty. You were already in your thirteenth sleep. I tiptoed down the stairs, trying not to be heard, but when I entered the kitchen... well... I caught him with a woman." My friend covered her face, embarrassed. "Zozo, I'm not a puritanical virgin, I've been with a few men, but that? He had her bent over the table, even with the dim light, it was clear how he was gripping her ass with his white knuckled fingers. Obviously, he saw me come in, I turned and ran, but I caught a glimpse of..."

Scarlett moved her hands, gesturing as if indicating the size of his member.

"Scar!" I let out a squeal, trying not to laugh.

"I'm a mess; I'm dying of embarrassment looking him in the face. — She shook her head. — With so many places in the house, did he really have to have sex right in the kitchen? In the kitchen?"

My friend looked extremely indignant.

"Maybe he didn't have time to get to the bedroom." A forced laugh escaped my mouth.

"Honestly? I could have lived without that image in my head. Now, I'm going to demand similar scenes from every man I sleep with." She shrugged.

"I don't mind if you want to hook up with my brother; after all, you already have the heart of his grandfather," I teased.

"Are you crazy? He's the same age as William. If one thinks he's too old, imagine the other." She rolled her eyes.

Every time my ex-governor's name was mentioned, I felt that pang in my heart. I didn't even check my phone frequently anymore, trying to avoid stumbling upon any news about him. I wanted to forget something that seemed to be growing stronger inside me.

"Have you picked out the car?" I asked impatiently.

"Yes, that one." She pointed to a car, running to the rack and grabbing the key.

CHAPTER THIRTY-FIVE

Zoey

"I read that taking the morning-after pill can delay your period," I declared, sitting on the toilet.

I had already done the quick test; it was on the bathroom counter. I had opened the suite door as soon as I finished so that Scarlett could be with me when the result came in.

"Let's hope that's the case," Scarlett said, not even looking at the stick.

I tapped my feet impatiently. We both knew the result should have been out by now, but neither of us had the courage to look.

"Do you want me to look, friend?" Scar asked.

I looked at the counter. The stick was facing down, hiding the result. I hoped I wasn't pregnant, although deep down, I knew I probably was. My period never delayed, and I was starting to have some odd symptoms, like excessive sleep and a heightened sense of smell, not enough to make me nauseous, just more acute with certain odors.

"Yes..." I nodded slightly, allowing her to see the result.

My friend picked up the stick, turning it towards her eyes. I lifted my face, wanting to see her reaction, and from her teary eyes, it was clear what the result was.

I bit my lip as tears began to well up in my eyes.

"Friend, it's positive," she whispered, and I instinctively placed my hand on my belly, as if hugging it tightly, wanting to protect the little one growing inside me.

"But it could be wrong, right?" I asked, still confused, trying to process if this was really happening.

"Friend, the box says 99.9% accuracy, and this is a super-positive. — Scar extended her hand, giving me the plastic stick with a small window showing two strong lines.

"What do I do now?" I asked, confused.

"I'd suggest you start by telling your brother, the hardest part first." The forced smile shone on her lips.

"You're right, although I need to prepare myself mentally..."

"Do you want me to be there with you?" Scar asked. "That way, if he tries to kill you, there will be witnesses."

"I think it's better." I smiled as genuinely as I could.

I lowered my gaze, looking at the test again. There were the two strong lines, confirming the positive result. Taking the morning-after pill 48 hours later apparently didn't work. Of all the mischief I've ever done in my life, this seemed to be the greatest of them all.

There was no way to process this quickly. I couldn't just walk out of there shouting that I was pregnant, that I might have a governor's child inside me, because that's not how things worked. Even if I wished it were different, it wouldn't be.

"AT THAT DINNER, I WAS so nervous that I couldn't eat properly, fearing my brother's reaction. What would he think? Just another problem for him. Was it time to return to California with my tail between my legs?"

After dinner, we went to the living room, where Ralph would probably invite my friend for a game of chess; those two matched better than they realized.

As I sat on the couch, I exchanged a quick glance with Scar, and she just nodded, making it clear that she would stand by me in this decision.

"Is something wrong, little sister?" Malcolm noticed my demeanor and sensed that something was off.

"Actually, yes," I said in a whisper, lifting my eyes to him. Malcolm was sitting on the couch across from me.

"Did something upset you? Was it one of my security guards?" In his protective manner, he immediately started asking several questions.

"No, it's not that," I said quickly. "It's just that... well... today Scar and I went out and stopped by a pharmacy in the mall."

Of course, we went to the pharmacy in the mall to throw off my brother's security guards, without them knowing anything.

"You're sick, why didn't you tell me?" There he was again, jumping to conclusions.

"No, brother, we went to the pharmacy to buy a pregnancy test," I blurted out in one breath. My brother's eyes widened, and he immediately looked at Scar before turning his gaze back to me.

"You're pregnant? Is that what you want to tell me? You're pregnant?" He stood up from the couch, pacing back and forth.

"Yes, the test was positive," I declared in an audible whisper.

Malcolm ran his hand through his dark hair, clenching his fists.

"Who's the father?" Even though he probably already knew the answer, he asked.

"William," I said, having just pronounced the name after days of not mentioning it.

"Of course, he had to ruin everything, even this," he roared.

The room fell silent; no one dared to speak, until Mr. Ralph cleared his throat and began to speak:

"My young lady, your brother is a bit impulsive and extremely protective. We have a trusted clinic; we'll ask them to come here tomorrow to take a blood sample so we can be sure that you're pregnant. We won't make any decisions in haste." The old man exchanged a long look with his grandson.

"Grandpa, she's pregnant, what do you want me to do?" The way he spoke was clearly mocking the situation, which could be seen as unfortunate to everyone involved.

"Ask her how she's doing, what she plans to do. I believe it's time for you to let Zoey make her own decisions without interfering in her life," Ralph said sincerely.

"Sister, what are you planning to do?" It seemed like Malcolm was the only man who would stop to listen and respect.

"I haven't had time to think about it. I found out about the pregnancy today. You were the first person I thought of telling, after Scar." Nervously, I began fidgeting with my fingers.

"Even though I hate that damn Fitzgerald right now, I think you need to tell him," my brother went straight to the source of the problem, the father of my child.

"I know, but how do I tell a man who didn't want children that I'm pregnant?" I forced a smile.

"If he doesn't accept it, you will always have me as your support..."

"I don't want him out of obligation or because of a pregnancy." I widened my eyes.

"Zozo, after we do the blood test, we'll think about the matter. From your expression, you're clearly exhausted. I want you to sleep and rest." Malcolm came towards me.

Just as Grandpa asked, he was being considerate. It was the support I needed for that moment, even though I wanted to punch William.

CHAPTER THIRTY-SIX

Zoey

Nervously, I bit the corner of my lip after the beta HCG test came back positive. There were no more doubts; now it was just a matter of an ultrasound to definitively confirm what we all already knew—I was pregnant.

"Are you sure everything is okay, friend?" Scar asked when we arrived at my parents' house.

"Yes, I couldn't stay in Springfield knowing that my life is here," I murmured with a sigh.

Malcolm walked right behind us. He refused to let me return alone, just like Scar did. The two of them seemed strangely close, as if they wanted to be near each other but weren't admitting it.

My friend opened the door of the house, motioning for me to go in first. My parents had already been informed of our arrival, and I headed straight to the living room where, upon seeing me, Mom got up from the sofa and practically threw herself into my arms.

"I missed my little girl," Mom whispered in the embrace.

"Mom," my voice was choked with emotion.

I missed her, our conversations, everything about California. Even though I loved being with my brother, my place was here, close to them.

I ran my hands over her back, feeling her warmth and all the maternal comfort. She was the kind of mother I wanted to reflect as the best mom I could be.

"Know that we're here for you, that you won't go through this alone." Holding my hand, we slowly pulled away.

I had asked Malcolm to tell them everything. I wanted them to know everything when we arrived so I wouldn't have to go through it all again, not to mention seeing their disappointed eyes. By doing this, we arrived at the house and I was already facing all the expressions of support or disapproval, but all I saw was their warmth.

"Thank you, Mom..." I sniffled, realizing I was more sensitive than usual.

My dad appeared beside me, placing his hand on my back.

"Even though I want to kill that damn Fitzgerald for what he did to my little girl..."

"Dad," I muttered. "No one forced me to do anything, just don't forget that."

It wasn't fair to place all the blame on him when I had been right there, enjoying everything.

"That's why we made this decision..." Just then, the doorbell rang.

"What decision?" I widened my eyes, feeling my heart race. I didn't know why, but that ringing made me realize it could be him.

Malcolm turned to answer the door. Great, they were hiding something from me. I met Scarlett's gaze, who just gave a sidelong smile. Yes, she also knew something I didn't.

The door closed, and my attentive ears tried to decipher who was coming in. But only footsteps were audible. I swallowed hard when my brother appeared next to William; it was clear how much Malcolm was controlling himself.

The Governor of California immediately directed his gaze toward me, and God, how I missed those blue eyes, the way he kept his attention on me for too long, unlike with anyone else.

After long seconds, he noticed that Scarlett was also there.

"Scarlett, what are you doing here? What do you want with me?" He seemed genuinely confused, not knowing what was going on.

William's voice was like an analgesic that pervaded my body. I took a few steps back, wanting to keep my distance from him, making sure I wouldn't weaken, not wanting to throw myself into the arms of the man who rejected me.

"Cousin, I'm just here to be a witness if any homicide were to occur," Scar said in her usual mocking tone.

"What?" William looked at Malcolm, and my brother narrowed his eyes at his old friend.

"Don't think I called you here to be friends again. You broke the biggest rule of our friendship," Malcolm roared.

"I know that very well. Did you call me here to rub it in my face again? Or to punch me?" William defended himself, taking a step to the side to distance himself from my brother.

"No, even though I'd love to give you another black eye, that's not why I called you."

William had no more bruises from the fight he had with my brother. The Governor looked at me and scanned my body, not with desire but with a concerned gesture, as if making sure I was okay.

"So what's the reason? Are you okay, little one?" He took a step toward me, only to be blocked by Malcolm, who wouldn't let him come closer.

The way he called me "little one" hurt, a pang of longing, a pain from something we experienced so briefly.

"Didn't we say to stay away from her?" my brother growled at him. "Know that you have no right to call her that."

"So just say it already, damn it! After all, you didn't invite me here for a cup of coffee, did you?" William was clearly starting to get worried.

"I'm pregnant," I said, catching everyone by surprise. Perhaps they didn't expect me to be the one to say it, but William's obvious agony made me uncomfortable.

Perhaps the way I said it wasn't the best, I didn't prepare the ground, I just said it, my eyes fixed on the Governor, wanting to see his reaction, which was one of horror, his eyes widening.

"Wh-what?" he stammered, maybe it was the first time I had seen him stutter.

"I'm pregnant, expecting a child of yours," I said, this time my statement was longer. I bit the corner of my lip, waiting for any reaction from him, whatever it might be.

"A child of mine?" William repeated.

"Yes," I whispered.

"How?" he seemed genuinely confused, not even knowing what to say.

"Do you really want to know how a child is conceived? I believe you should know very well," it was my father who spoke this time, making his presence known.

"Yes... of course I know." William kept his eyes on me, not caring that there were two men there wanting to skin him alive. "What I don't understand is how?"

"I don't use any contraceptive method; you didn't ask me, and I forgot...," it was strange to talk about this topic with my parents present. "I took the morning-after pill... but not in time, only two days later. I thought it would work, but it didn't. The fault isn't yours..."

"No! I mean, of course, it is." William's reaction made me look at him again. I expected him to reject me once more. "If you're pregnant, the blame will never be yours."

He wasn't rejecting me? The Governor was, for the first time, not rejecting me?

CHAPTER THIRTY-SEVEN

William

I had nowhere to hold on to, not even a wall behind me to search for something to prevent myself from falling apart.

Everyone there hated me, expected me to do something. I was at a disadvantage; what could I say when any word out of place could make Malcolm leap at me and want a new physical confrontation?

The silence in the room made everyone wait for a word from me, when all I wanted was to kill my longing for that little one, hold her in my arms, feel her warmth, hear the most outrageous words from her mouth.

My last few days had been a true hell.

When Malcolm called me, I knew it wasn't for anything good, that no apology would come. However, my greatest fear was something concerning her, Zoey. He didn't tell me anything, just forced me to come to his parents' house.

And there I was, receiving the news that she was pregnant, expecting a child of mine.

Of all the things that had crossed my mind, that had never crossed it. A child? A child of hers and mine? I had always wanted to be a father, but in no way did I think it would be like this, receiving the news like this, with a woman who wasn't even mine. Not mine because I didn't want her, or rather, it was how I wanted to think, considering there wasn't a damn day I didn't think about Zoey Beaumont.

"What do you want from me? I can't approach her. What do you want from me?" I questioned, knowing I was at a complete disadvantage.

"We want you to know the mess you've made," Malcolm growled beside me.

Clearly, I wouldn't have his friendship anytime soon. Malcolm harbored an unparalleled anger, and maybe what I had done was unforgivable. But the thing was, I didn't regret what I had done, I didn't regret holding Zoey in my arms.

"Mess? At what point could I call my future child, your nephew, a mess?" I growled, turning my face and clenching my fists.

"You know I didn't call the child a mess, but what you did to her." Malcolm took a step toward me, but this time I didn't retaliate, taking another step toward him. I wouldn't be caught off guard again; if anyone left with a black eye, it wouldn't be me.

"I don't regret what I did at all," my words clearly made Malcolm even angrier.

"Enough! Please, enough! You should act like two adults, not like animals about to claw each other again," Zoey said, raising her voice, making everyone look at her. "Once and for all, understand, I wasn't forced by Mr. Fitzgerald to do anything. I'm not some helpless little girl. If I'm pregnant, it's not just his consequence, but mine as well. Now, what we're going to do about it, I don't know. I just ask, you two were always best friends, can't you forget this?"

She seemed to be begging with a stamp of her foot, her eyes filled with tears.

"No, Zozo, there's no way to forget that this traitor seduced my sister!"

"For God's sake, Malcolm, no one was seduced," it seemed like the little one wanted to mend our friendship, but after everything, I thought it would be practically impossible.

"If there's a child growing inside her, all I can do for them is offer my full support," I said, making it clear that I wanted Zoey.

"What do you mean?" Carl, her father, and Zoey questioned.

The little one, in her mother's arms, looked at me anxiously. She had an exhausted expression, dark circles under her eyes that had always been bright with joy, her slightly plump lips set rigid without any sign of happiness.

"I mean I want to marry Zoey and thus take on my responsibility as a father," I said firmly, doing what any man in my position would do.

"No! I won't marry you." Zoey's eyes widened as if what I had said was absurd. "I won't marry just because of the child growing inside me. You've given countless reasons to prove how wrong I was to be by your side, my age is still the same, I'm still much younger, and I'm still Malcolm's sister, your best friend..."

"Ex," Malcolm cut her off, making it clear he didn't want my friendship.

"What do you want from me, then? I can't approach you if your guard dog here will want to attack me. I can't claim my own child, hell! What do you want me to do?" I growled, running my hand through my hair in frustration.

"Simple, you have until her belly starts to show to win my daughter over," Carl said, making me look in his direction.

"And if I don't succeed?" I wanted to know all the possibilities.

"You'll have to deal with the consequences of being a single father in the face of your career, which we know is important." That made me swallow hard.

A pregnancy with a woman who wasn't mine could be an electoral scandal. What I needed to do was win Zoey over, make her mine, marry her, and thus acknowledge the pregnancy. I'd have a stable family, and my voters would see the perfect family image they wanted.

"So, do I have the opportunity to win her over?" I asked, waiting for her father's approval.

"Yes, you have my consent," Carl nodded.

But his consent meant nothing if the little one didn't want me close. I looked at Zoey, waiting for her response.

Once again, silence fell, everyone waiting for Zoey to say something. I had never been so nervous, not even when I was elected Governor of California. It was as if, despite all her insistence on me, I had finally received what no one else had before, my full attention.

"Brother?" She looked at Malcolm, as if asking for his permission. But damn, I was jealous, jealous that she had run to him and not to me, as if he were her first person, something I wanted to be.

"I agree with Dad, but the decision of what to do is yours. It's a decision that needs to be only yours, Zozo."

Finally, her black eyes met mine. She was nervous, blinking rapidly.

"Ah... okay, I think I want to give you this opportunity, an opportunity to apologize, redeem yourself, and show that you deserve my trust," she said firmly with her decision, as if she already knew what she was going to do but just needed her father and brother as her protectors.

That was for a short time, because soon, it would be me!

CHAPTER THIRTY-EIGHT

William

"We can schedule a day to talk. I'm tired from the trip right now. I didn't know you'd be here," Zoey said, making it clear she didn't want my presence.

This was a surprise to me; everything about that woman was a mystery.

And there was nothing I could say or do in front of her family. Everyone there hated me. A word out of place, a lewd suggestion to seduce her, would provoke Malcolm and Carl.

"Yes, we can talk another time," I said, knowing that on top of everything, I needed to process the news of becoming a father.

I wasn't expecting this; I'm going to be a father, damn it!

At the same time that I wanted to embrace that woman, I wanted to scream to everyone how happy I was.

"Scarlett, do you want to come with me?" I looked at my cousin, knowing she was at Malcolm's house with Zoey.

"Yes, do you need me, friend?" she asked, concerned.

"No, I'm fine." That was the first time I saw Zoey flash a brief smile.

Damn, knowing I had all those smiles before and didn't value them.

"Let's go then. I want to stay at your parents' house since mine moved to Washington DC." She playfully rolled her eyes. "It seems I'm no longer the favorite."

"You lose badly to Sadie's toothless grin," I joked with my cousin.

"You can't compete with my beautiful niece, especially now that another one is on the way," she referred to Zachary's second daughter.

Before I turned away, I glanced at the little one. She wasn't crying anymore but still had tear marks on her face. I wished I could go to her, comfort her, and tell her that I didn't want her next to me just because of the pregnancy, but all that was my fault because I let her believe it was because of the pregnancy, when I hadn't wanted her before.

"Shall we go, Will?" Scar called, pulling me out of my reverie, and I blinked a few times.

"I'm sorry, Zoey," was all I could manage before turning and following my cousin.

We left the Beaumont residence together. My driver was waiting for me, the door open for me to enter, followed by my cousin. I looked back at the house as the car pulled away and instructed the driver to head straight to my parents' condominium.

"Are you okay, cousin?" Scarlett asked suddenly.

"Okay wouldn't be the word to describe me right now." I forced a crooked smile. "After all, I'm going to be a father, and that's all I know."

"Were you with her when she found out about the pregnancy?" Scar also smiled sincerely.

"And how did she react?" I wanted to know more about that moment.

"You're lucky her parents sent you the message. Zoey is quite lost, stunned. My friend didn't expect this news," which made me feel like a monster.

"I didn't know. It was really my mistake to think she was on any contraceptive...," my voice trailed off.

"Yes, cousin, it was a major mistake. Zoey may have her flaws, but she always saw you as a prince in her mind, and she didn't really think when she was in your arms. Now, you both need to figure out what to do."

"Just tell me something, does she still feel the same about me? Or did I screw up so badly that I have no chance anymore?" I asked, needing to know that I hadn't completely lost her.

"Zozo still likes you, but she's very disappointed. It was a huge shock. She didn't even want to mention your name." She gave a half-smile.

"But she was here today, in front of me," I said, trying to find some explanation.

"Zoey didn't know you would be here because Malcolm knows his sister and knew she would delay confronting the father of her child. You know her brother; he wants to resolve everything *right* now." My cousin shrugged.

I knew exactly what she meant; I knew that man very well.

"Has she had any ultrasounds yet?"

"Not yet. She'll schedule one in the coming days."

"I want to be there..."

"Cousin, you know that showing up at an obstetric clinic might not be well received," she stated the obvious.

"Damn it, I want to be involved in her pregnancy," I growled, feeling helpless.

"Take it easy. You can start by giving her a gift tomorrow. It's Zoey's birthday; she's turning twenty." I suddenly turned to Scar.

"Really?" I flashed a brief smile. "That's a perfect opportunity."

"Do you know what to get her?" My cousin looked at me suspiciously.

I know Zoey loves to draw; after all, she works with her parents at the art gallery. I know she loves flowers; all women do, right?

"Do you know what her favorite flowers are?" I asked, curious.

"White roses. She always said she liked their shape, how they seem shy and delicate," Scarlett answered promptly. "Is that all you're giving? Flowers are so generic, Will..."

"No, Scarlett Fitzgerald, the rest is a secret," I teased my cousin, rolling my eyes.

We spent the rest of the ride talking, with Scar mentioning her stay at Malcolm's house and revealing a bit about old Ross's health. Surprisingly, she only had praise for Ralph, which was a shock since every time I went to his house, he was in a bad mood.

The car stopped in front of my parents' house, and I got out with my cousin.

"Are you going to tell them now?" Scar wanted to know.

"I think it's better to. I'm pretty sure if they don't hear it from me, they'll hear it soon enough from Claire. We know Mom and Zoey's mom like to chat," I said, stating what we both already knew.

We entered my parents' house, just as my father came out of the kitchen, looking at me with a confused expression.

"Son, what are you doing here at this time of day?" he asked, puzzled.

"Let's go to the living room. I want to talk to Mom and you," I said, knowing my brother wasn't home, so I didn't call him.

Nodding, my father followed us, giving my cousin a hug. Everyone considered her the little princess of the family.

"Dear, hello," my mother greeted me. After days of calling me William, she had returned to calling me "dear."

It was hard for everyone to forget what I had done, and now it seemed they were about to remember everything again.

"Well..." I clasped my hands together while Scar took a seat on the sofa, clearly showing her support. My parents looked at me, seated side by side, not understanding. "We were just at the Beaumont residence. Zoey is back with her family..."

"Oh, what a blessing, Claire, I missed my daughter so much," Mom interrupted, clapping excitedly. "But what were you doing there? Weren't you fighting?"

She looked at me, confused.

"If you let me continue..." I forced a nervous smile. "What I have to say is a bit confusing and might catch you off guard. I just want you to listen and know that I'll do my best to make everything work. Zoey is pregnant, expecting a child of mine."

My father quickly got up from the sofa, and my mother covered her mouth with her hand, tears welling up in her eyes. It was clearly what she wanted, but behind it all was my political career, to which I had dedicated my whole life.

CHAPTER THIRTY-NINE

Zoey

To say I slept well that night would be a bold-faced lie. I couldn't close my eyes, all that confusion, the anxiety about the pregnancy, not knowing what to think.

I hadn't expected William's reaction, didn't even know what to expect from him, but surely, it wasn't anything like what he showed.

I sat slowly on my bed, rubbing my eyes, the exhaustion taking over me. It felt like a two-ton truck had run over me.

I reached for my phone beside the bed and was puzzled by the notification from an unknown number. There was no way to reply to the message since it was from a private number.

"*Happy birthday, my little whirlwind. I wish I could be by your side on this day. After all, it's not every day you turn twenty...*
With love, your William"

My William? *My?*

I stared at that message for long seconds. For God's sake, I really didn't expect that. For years, it was all I wanted, a message from William, and now I had it, exactly in the form I always wanted.

Your William, I read that part again, my foolish heart missing a beat. Warming up with the feeling that he wanted me to be his.

He even remembered my birthday, or believed that Scarlett must have mentioned it, after all, my friend wanted her cousin to get his act together.

"Dear?" A knock on the door made me look up.

"Come in, Mom." I locked my phone.

My mom entered the room, her eyes locking onto mine.

"Happy birthday, my dear," she said with a twinkle in her eye. "My little girl is turning twenty."

"And pregnant," I said softly.

"With a baby, I'm going to be a grandma." My mom sat on the edge of my bed and gave me a tight hug.

It was strange how much I desired that baby, even knowing that I was young, that I had a whole life ahead of me. Knowing that a new little person was growing inside me made all that emotional turmoil worth it.

"My daughter, how are you feeling? About everything, about this pregnancy, about William? We haven't even had time to talk properly." My mom took my hands, caressing them.

"It's everything I've always wanted, *you know*? William, a child, working at the gallery with you, but I feel like something's not right, it's out of order. William rejected me, and it hurt, Mom." I gave a sidelong smile. "He sent me a birthday message, and my heart melted. How can I still be all soft for the man who rejected me? How do I feel like I love that man? Shouldn't I hate him?"

"Love isn't always simple; often, it's complicated, takes turns we don't even understand." Mom made me blink several times to hold back my tears. "I know you still love the governor. A love like yours doesn't disappear overnight. That man is very lucky to have your heart."

Her fingers brushed beneath my eyes, drying a single tear that had fallen.

"Thank you, Mom." I ran my hand through my hair, pulling it into a bun on top of my head.

"Abigail knew today was your birthday and asked if she could throw a birthday dinner for you at her house." My mom got up from the bed, her eyes curious as they looked at me.

"Does she know about the pregnancy?" I asked.

"Yes, William told her."

I nodded. If he had told her, it meant he was taking everything seriously, without faltering. Something I had noticed in the last few days I spent in Springfield at my brother's house was that I hadn't seen any news about him with another woman; he was even mentioned in all of them as *Governor William Fitzgerald was alone...*

Which was a novelty for him.

What was the reason for doing that? So many unanswered questions.

"What do you think, my dear? Do you feel comfortable going?" My mom asked again after my silence.

"I think it'll be nice." I gave a big smile. "After all, I've always liked all the Fitzgeralds."

I slid one foot at a time off the bed and stood up.

"Honey, you need to sleep. You have deep circles under your eyes, you need to think about the little one growing inside you." Mom was worried.

"I slept very poorly last night." I sighed, shrugging my shoulders.

"I'm sure you did. Look at your face." She ran her hand under my eyes.

"If possible, I'll lie down for a bit in the afternoon and take a nap." I smiled sideways, trying to calm her.

"If possible? No, you are going to sleep..."

"I missed this." I wrapped my arms around her waist, giving her a hug.

"Now tell me, I thought you had blocked the governor's number. Did you unblock it?" she asked as we left the room.

I was wearing one of my pink pajamas.

"It's still blocked, but he must have messaged me from one of his other confidential phones." I shrugged my shoulders. "Wow, that smell is divine, I'm so hungry."

The aroma of breakfast filled the whole house, making me salivate with hunger.

"There's a gift that arrived for you this morning." My mom pointed to the sofa and a large bouquet of white flowers, my favorites.

Mom said it was a somewhat strange taste, but I loved them. I smiled widely.

"Was it you guys?" I asked, quickly descending the stairs.

"No, there's a note inside, and another gift box next to it."

My mom followed me into the living room. I picked up the bouquet, smelling the perfect flowers, and took the envelope out.

I sat on the sofa, placing the flowers beside me. I opened the delicate card, seeing the handwritten calligraphy inside:

"Little one, not all the roses in the world could express the joy I felt upon learning you were pregnant, expecting our child. I know I made many barriers between us, and I deeply regret it. The taste of regret is anything but sweet, and I'm feeling it acutely. I hope you can forgive me one day, forgive all my mistakes, and finally be happy. Happy birthday, my little whirlwind. Your William F."

Once again, there was "your" twice in one day—how to deal with all this?

I wiped under my eyes, drying the tear that had fallen for the second time.

"That's also from him, dear." Mom pointed to the box.

I turned, tearing open the wrapping to find a set of paints—my favorite brand, with the hardest-to-find shades, and new brushes. I picked one up and felt the texture, seeing the emblem of the model I had been dying *to* buy, which was no longer in production as it was an exclusive line.

"Good heavens, how did he get all this?" I looked up at Mom.

"I admit I was an accomplice, but I didn't know he would get those brushes. I'm a bit jealous now. He called asking about the paint brands you used and something that was impossible for you to have. Jokingly, I mentioned this set of brushes." Mom reached out and picked one up.

"They're perfect, Mom, look at the lightness, the contrast." I kept twirling them in my hand.

For God's sake, how did he manage to do all this? Now I was both curious and grateful, as I had wanted all this so much. And once again, William managed to surprise me. If this was his remorseful version, it was surpassing all my expectations.

CHAPTER FORTY

Zoey

I wore one of my favorite dresses, a light blue one, and completed the look with high heels that made me a little taller.

I couldn't even manage to do anything with my hair, as I was too nervous for that. When I left my room, my mom was already waiting for me, along with Dad.

Malcolm had to return to Springfield; he couldn't stay here for too long with things *to* do in his city.

It didn't take a psychic to know that William would also be present at the dinner. Even with all those wonderful flowers and the painting kit I couldn't stop drooling over, I had ended up testing the brushes with the new paints. Everything was incredible; the governor had hit the mark precisely with that gift. But I hadn't unlocked his number; William needed far more than a gift I loved to get my number freed.

My dad didn't like using drivers, so most of the time when we went out, he always drove.

During the whole trip to the Fitzgerald house, they talked about paintings to be displayed in the gallery, while I nervously stared out the window, running one finger over the other.

After long minutes in the car, we arrived at the family's condominium and stopped in front of the house.

I opened my door, stepping out with Mom, who gave me a look of affection.

"Are you okay, dear?" She clearly thought I might lose it at any moment when, in reality, I didn't even know what to think.

"Yes, Mom, I'm fine." I smiled back and we walked toward the door. By the garage, I recognized William's security guards standing there.

We hadn't even knocked when Abigail opened the door, looking directly at me.

"My angel." She opened her arms for a hug, and of course, I returned the gesture, patting William's mother's back. "I'm so glad you're back."

"I'm glad too," I whispered.

"It's your birthday, but we're the ones getting the gift." She stepped back, brushing her hands over my arms. "How are you? The most important thing is your mental health."

"Strangely, well." I gave her a sincere smile. "Though a bit confused."

"That's normal, after all, everything happened so quickly, didn't it?" Abigail rubbed my back, guiding me inside.

As I entered the room, my eyes immediately focused on him, the governor, who was sitting next to his brother, Sawyer, who was showing him something on his phone.

William looked up and locked eyes with me. It was clear that we wanted to talk, to communicate, but it was as if there was something between us, blocking us. Perhaps it was the way we ended our last meeting.

"So, I'm going to have a nephew." Sawyer made me look at him with his most exaggerated manner of speaking.

"Less, Saw," William grumbled, but his brother paid him no mind.

Coming toward me without even asking permission, Sawyer, who looked much like William in size and appearance, gave me a strong hug, speaking softly in my ear:

"I've always believed in the crazy ones." Obviously, he was joking, making me let out a weak laugh.

"Did you just call me crazy?" I pulled away, raising my eyes to show I understood he was joking.

"A little crazy in a good way." He winked flirtatiously.

Sawyer was much more outgoing than William. Perhaps if I had liked him, I wouldn't have had so many disappointments. But liking the difficult one seemed like a bigger way to torment myself.

"Enough, Sawyer." I looked up to see the governor, who I hadn't even noticed had come closer.

"Calm down, little brother, I'm not going to steal your girl." Sawyer rolled his eyes, stepping away from me, but not without winking at me first.

"Can we talk privately?" William asked, unsure if he could touch me.

"*Oh*, yes," I agreed, watching him point to the outside of the house.

My friend was sitting on the sofa, talking to her uncle. Scarlett would return to campus the next day.

We went through the back door, and the yard was lit by ground lights. We stopped next to the pool where there was a glass table for anyone who wanted to sit and watch those swimming. It was all so beautiful.

Nervous, I stood a good distance from William, allowing myself to look into his eyes.

"I think starting by apologizing for our last meeting would be too boring, wouldn't it?" He bit his lip, extending his hand to hold my fingers.

I knew William couldn't stand being without physical contact for too long. His warm touch on mine sparked tiny flames, making me realize how much I missed it.

"Little one," he whispered when he noticed I wasn't going to say anything.

"Yes, William." I didn't pull my hand away; I let him see how far he would go, or at least how long I could stay resistant.

"Happy birthday," his voice was low, resonating within me like a song that left me ecstatic. "I hope you liked the gift."

It was impossible not to smile, impossible to stay indifferent to everything around me, remembering the gift he had given me.

"Thank you, I loved it," I declared, unable to contain my curiosity. "I was crazy looking for those brushes, how did you manage to get them?"

"I have my sources." He flashed one of his beautiful smiles.

"I know several suppliers, and I still couldn't get them." I squinted my eyes slightly.

"Let's just say I contacted the manufacturer directly; the perks of the last name." He winked flirtatiously.

"Was it because of Chris?"

"I just mentioned I was the president's cousin, and it took two touches to get what I wanted." He shrugged his shoulders.

"I truly loved them; I even tested them, they're even more perfect." I said, enchanted, noticing the governor had been looking at my face for too long. "The way you're looking at me is frightening..."

My sentence faltered as William's smile widened.

"I'm just enchanted; I thought I'd never see your smile again."

"You hit my soft spot, I love painting," I replied, pulling my hand away and surprising him when he realized I had broken our touch.

"On a scale from one to ten, how angry are you with me?" he asked.

"I'm not angry with you; it's more like hurt. The way you rejected me, let me go, didn't fight for me... and now, everything seems so easy, you decided you want me, it feels forced," I spoke what came from the bottom of my heart.

"It really does seem that way, but I promise I'll make you realize it's the opposite of what you think." He tried to take my hand again, but I pulled it away, resentfully.

I turned my face when I heard the clacking of heels; it was Scar.

"Dinner is served, lovebirds can come in." She let out a mocking laugh.

"Your humor cheers me up, friend," I teased, leaving William behind as she went with her.

It was hard, it hurt. I wanted to give in to him, but there was something inside me that kept me from future pain, just as he had already caused.

CHAPTER FORTY-ONE

Zoey

Dinner was lively, of course, with my pregnancy being the main focus. Talking about the baby made everything feel more real.

"Tomorrow will be my first appointment with the obstetrician," I finally said, wiping my mouth with the napkin as I finished eating.

"Promise you'll record everything and show me the video of our little bean, okay?" Scar clapped her hands excitedly.

"Of course," I nodded, smiling at her.

"Who's going to accompany you?" William's voice was heard.

"My mother," I replied to him.

"I would like to go with you," he said, drawing all eyes to himself.

"I don't know if that would be the best choice," William's father said, looking worried.

"You yourself said you never missed a single one of Mom's appointments." He raised an eyebrow, convinced.

"It's different; they were married," I declared, drawing attention to myself.

"It would be even simpler if you decided to marry me. We already have a child, we had a brief affair, we get along well, what's the problem?" The governor seemed to be losing his patience.

"What's the problem?" I questioned mockingly. "You are the problem, William. I spent years of my life being a foolish girl in love with you, always making it clear that everyone came first and I was last.

Our last meeting was a disaster. Remember when you said my age was a problem? A problem for your precious political career?"

I slammed my hands on the table, losing all my patience.

"Fuck my career, what matters now is you, Zoey! Do you want me to resign? Do you want me to give up everything and just stick to my family's business? I would do that for you, damn it! Is that what you wanted to hear? I'll do whatever you want." He stood up from his chair, his breathing rapid and heavy.

"Then do it." I also stood up from my chair, speaking in the heat of the moment.

A silence fell over the room; maybe no one expected that reaction, not even me. I gripped the table harder, as if everything in front of me was spinning, a hazy veil forming in my eyes, until everything suddenly went dark.

I SQUEEZED MY EYES shut, slowly opening my eyelids. The ceiling was white; I turned my face slowly and saw my mother sitting with a worried look in my direction.

Feeling discomfort in my hand, I looked up to see a tube connected to an IV drip.

"Mom, what happened?" I whispered, worried.

"Dear." She quickly got up and came to me, forcing a smile as tears rolled down her cheeks.

"Mommy, why are you crying?" I began to panic.

All I remembered was arguing with William, and after that, everything became a blur.

"Oh, my angel, I'm just relieved, happy..." She lowered herself, placing her hand on my shoulders and hugging me.

I was even more confused.

"Mommy, why are you crying, please tell me?" I asked, seeing her press a button on the bed.

"Don't worry, I'm just calling the doctor. She said to call her as soon as you woke up." She gave a loving smile but revealed nothing.

I wanted to ask again, to demand an explanation, but the door opened and a woman walked in. She held a tablet in her hand and came toward me. The white coat made it clear she was my doctor.

"Miss Beaumont," she said, looking at the monitor with some indicators of my health status.

"Can someone please tell me what happened?" My impatience was evident.

My eyes met the doctor's, who nodded. Before she started speaking, she performed a few quick tests, asking what day it was and more, proving that I was okay.

"Am I able to know now? I'm not pregnant, right? Did I lose my baby?" Suddenly, my eyes filled with tears.

Thinking that made my mind race, my heart tighten. I was beginning to adjust to the idea of being a mother, already imagining a little one of mine and William's. I wanted that baby deeply, and the thought of losing something I might never have had was painful.

"We needed to put you on IV with some painkillers and sleeping aids so you could rest," the doctor began. "Your mother mentioned you hadn't been sleeping well, and perhaps the exhaustion led to the fainting spell. We did a brief ultrasound with your mother present, and the baby is approximately six weeks along, based on your last menstrual period, as your mother provided. The baby appears healthy, with the right measurements for this stage of development. It's too early to hear the heartbeat, which is normal for this gestational period. I recommend another ultrasound in two weeks, but your obstetrician will provide more details."

Hearing about my pregnancy was a relief. I was indeed pregnant; a baby was growing inside me.

"We'll keep you under observation tonight to monitor your condition," the doctor said with a kind nod.

Turning away, the doctor left. I turned my gaze back to my mother.

"Did you see the ultrasound, Mom? How was it?" I wanted more information about my baby.

"It was amazing." She started to tear up again.

"There's more, isn't there? Did something happen? Where's William?" I looked around as if he might appear by magic.

"Dealing with the media," it wasn't necessary to question why, to know the reason for him dealing with that.

"Is it very serious?"

"Yes," she confirmed, nodding.

"Oh, heavens," I murmured, worried.

"Maybe nothing would have happened, but the governor lost his temper. Your father even had to calm him down. William wouldn't let anyone else carry you until we arrived at the hospital, and when we got there, he lost the rest of his patience because of a two-minute delay. I've never seen a Fitzgerald in that state; the man was distraught. He said exactly this: 'If anything happens to my wife and my child, I'll make sure to replace the entire staff of this place.'"

I widened my eyes. William shouldn't have said that; his cousins must have been freaking out.

"I... I... don't even know what to say," I whispered, alarmed.

"Fortunately, no one recorded a video, but it was broadcasted in the news, and now everyone wants to know more about the woman beside the governor, and well, he's announcing her as his fiancée..."

"He what?" Great, now everything was a complete mess.

CHAPTER FORTY-TWO

William

Zoey would want my head when she found out what I'd done. She had explicitly stated that she wanted to regain all her trust in me before we publicly announced our child. And I had just done the exact opposite of what she asked.

I turned my body to find my father standing there after briefly speaking with my aunt's journalist friend. There were many at the hospital entrance, but since he was close to Aunt Natalie, I ended up giving him that information.

What could cause more trouble in my life was the fact that I had lied.

I didn't want her name exposed as the girl who wanted to have the governor's child, so I decided to lie to protect Zoey's image. I said that we became involved after my engagement ended, that it was something private because we were getting to know each other well and wanted to see if we would work out. But a wonderful unforeseen event happened—her pregnancy. Those were the words I used.

But now there was another major issue: explaining all of this to Zoey.

"She's awake," my father said, and I finally breathed a sigh of relief. "Your mother said she's talking, conscious."

"Can I see her?" I asked, walking beside him down the hospital corridor.

I had lost all control; I shouldn't have reacted that way, ordering them to take care of my girl as quickly as possible. I lost all my composure, and the mistake was entirely mine. My fear spoke volumes; I couldn't lose that woman. Seeing her like that in my arms made me feel a fear like I had never felt before.

"Your mother said she wants to see you, and Claire has already told her everything that happened, even about you spreading that you're engaged." I ran my hand through my hair, worried.

"I hope she at least lets me explain," I whispered with a sigh.

"Well, that's what we hope for." Dad stopped walking. "This is the room where Zoey is."

I nodded, knocked twice on the door, opened it, and peered inside. There was my little one, lying on that hospital bed with all those wires attached to her.

"Can I come in?" I asked before entering.

Zoey nodded, and her mother, who was there, kissed her daughter's face and left. My mother must have been there too, so my father knew what had happened.

I walked around the room, standing next to her. We were alone, which might make it easier to explain things.

"Before anything, can I explain myself?" I started, not wanting to ruin everything.

"Go ahead, fiancé," she said with irony, not in a good way.

"I lost my head, I felt fear like I had never felt before, a deep fear. You were unconscious; no matter what we tried, nothing woke you from that fainting spell. I was terrified, I couldn't lose you, and I ended up ordering them to take care of you as quickly as possible. Maybe I shouldn't have spoken that way, but I couldn't lose you, Zoey," I said with complete sincerity.

"But why did you lie about us? Why didn't you tell the truth?"

"Simple. You know how the media is; they would have placed all the blame on you, as if you had deliberately caused the pregnancy. I would never allow your name to be splashed across every magazine as the culprit, when you were nothing of the sort. So I decided to lie; I said that after my engagement ended, we started to get to know each other, and since we were from the same family, everything became easier. We didn't want to talk about our relationship until we were sure of our feelings. But a surprise caught us off guard—a baby to bring us even closer together," I revealed everything.

"You're really saying that you did all this to protect me?" She squinted at me.

"Yes, I would never let anything happen to you and our child." My eyes focused on her hand where the IV was attached.

"And what about my age, which was always a problem for you?" Zoey was still on the defensive.

"Really? I cared about it because I thought it was wrong for a 38-year-old man like me, who has experienced everything, to tie a beautiful girl like you to my side. Do you understand? Do you get that you're too young for me?" I asked vehemently, seeking her answer.

"Yes, William, I understand, and it was never a problem for me," she said firmly. "And what about your voters, what will they think?"

"I might end up in a bad light with all of them, but I no longer care. I finally want to live something outside the norm, something different from what I'm always used to and strictly following. If they can't accept that a man can get involved with his ex-best friend's sister, they will never want my happiness." Our eyes locked, clearly showing that for the first time, we were having a sensible conversation.

"I didn't want your friendship to be affected; sometimes I feel guilty about it," she whispered, and I immediately took her hand.

"Never feel that way." Zoey lowered her face, examining my hand over hers.

"What will we do now? After all, you just revealed that we're engaged and having a child, all in a rushed manner..." Her sentence trailed off as if she was searching for strength to speak.

"I want you to move in with me, I want to marry you..."

"William, you're being hasty again with all this; I don't want a marriage like this. I don't want us to marry prematurely, without feeling, without love. That's not the type of union I dreamed of." Zoey pulled her hand away distrustfully.

"Then come live with me, so we can say we're engaged, even if we're not. I'll be able to accompany you to appointments and will patiently wait for every decision you make..."

"And that you'll try to seduce me every day you're by my side," she cut in with a small smile.

"I admit that it's almost impossible not to do that. Will you come live with me? Let's see if we work well together, leaving our age and everything that separates us behind. Just living a life together," I pleaded, focusing on Zoey's delicate face.

Her black hair was loose over her shoulders, her dark circles still there. The girl who was always lively, cheerful, and smiling now had something that seemed to leave her disheartened, or perhaps it was just exhaustion.

"Please, little one," I practically begged.

"Okay, you win. Maybe this life together will be good." The smile Zoey gave me relieved me.

CHAPTER FORTY-THREE

Zoey

We had to leave through the hospital's back door so we wouldn't be seen.

William sat next to me, and after discussing it extensively, we decided that it was best to go to William's house, which was more secluded and where photographers wouldn't be able to invade our privacy.

Mom said she would send all my painting supplies there so that I would have something to occupy my time.

Everyone was concerned about my health, to the point that I even ended up in the emergency room.

According to the doctor, it was just a scare, but rest and stress-free environment were necessary.

"You know you'll need to give me my phone at some point, right?" I asked, looking at William, who was at that moment fiddling with his own device.

"I'm not sure if that would be good for you," he said, looking up with concern.

"I'm stronger than you think." I shrugged.

"Then I'll hand it over, but I want to be by your side every time you use it..."

"William." I sighed heavily. "I can handle this kind of thing."

"I just want to look out for you..."

"Is it worse than what they said about Savannah?" I asked, recalling the time Zachary's wife was the target of millions accusing her of being opportunistic.

"Not really. In fact, the news isn't bad, but if you dig deep, there might be some unpleasant comments." I shook my head at what he said.

"Then I can handle it, seriously," I said with conviction. "I'd rather know than have to put a blindfold on and pretend nothing is happening."

William, after staring at me for a long moment, reached inside his jacket and pulled out my phone. Even though he was hesitant, he handed it to me.

"Promise that any sign of distress you'll call me?" he asked as I took the phone.

"Yes," I agreed, taking the phone in my hand.

I pressed the power button. It didn't take long for the phone to restart, and the notifications started pouring in non-stop. Since I was active on social media, most came from there. Many tags, but I decided not to look at them at that moment. I only opened my messages from people close to me.

I responded to a few friends, reassuring them, even with my head down I could feel William's gaze on me. Finally, I turned off the phone and looked back at him.

"See, it wasn't a big deal." I widened my smile.

"Yes," was all he said.

After a few minutes, I saw the condo, the same one where we had our last meeting.

"No photographers?" I asked, surprised by the fact.

"They must all be at my penthouse as I expected." He gave me a sidelong smile.

"That makes sense." I let out a relieved sigh.

There were only a few houses, spaced apart with a vast yard separating them. It was the perfect place to start a family.

"The last time we were here, we..."

"The last time we were here, I said many things I shouldn't have. You're beautiful, and know that I'm immensely happy to have you here by my side. I know it's difficult, but I promise to make you forget all the bad things I said that day," William cut in as the car stopped in front of his house.

"But now you want? Do you want to build your family here with me?" My door was opened as I asked.

We got out, and the governor walked around the car to my side.

"Yes, Zoey, I want to build our family," the way he spoke was sincere, but always seemed connected to something sudden.

I felt his fingers intertwine with mine, but I didn't pull away, just let it be. We stopped in front of the house, and he typed in a code to unlock the door.

I walked in, recognizing it as it was the last time I was there—large, luxurious, and cozy.

I took off my flats and went barefoot. The governor removed his jacket and unbuttoned the top buttons of his shirt.

"This, this..." I stammered, unable to find the right words. "It feels like a dream, a dream that makes me afraid to wake up..."

He stopped unbuttoning at that moment, standing in front of me, holding my chin.

"I know it took me too long to realize the wonderful woman you've become. Know that not a single day went by that I didn't think of you, your dark eyes, the beautiful way you smile." His thumb traced along my cheek. "Zoey, you were the only woman who has been in my arms here in this house and anywhere else since that day."

"Are you saying you haven't been with anyone else? That I was your last?" That was news to me, but William nodded in confirmation. "Not even kisses, caresses, nothing?"

Maybe the way I asked made him smile, a smirk appearing on his lips.

"Nothing. My thoughts were all on you, wanting to know how you were, missing you completely. I never thought I could miss someone as much as I missed you," he said, his face moving closer to mine.

My legs felt like jelly, softened by the governor's words. I bit my lip nervously, not breaking my gaze from him, and let the gentle touch of his lips brush against mine as his thumb caressed my chin.

It wasn't a kiss, just a lingering peck that drew a sigh from my lips.

"I missed this so much, your scent, your taste, your lips that are as soft as touching the clouds," he murmured without pulling away.

"Have you ever touched a cloud, governor?" I asked with a hint of sarcasm.

"No, but I'm sure it must be something like your lips." Slowly, I started to pull away, knowing that was my limit. Any further move might end up throwing me into his arms.

"I could easily get spoiled," I said, looking around.

"Where will I stay, after all? We agreed not to share the same bed," I wanted to change the subject quickly.

"I think that's a big mistake. I could watch over you while you sleep, put you to bed, make sure my girl is sleeping well." He gave a brief, mischievous smile.

"If I didn't know you well, I might believe that, but I do know you, William," I called his name with a teasing tone.

"I thought it might work out. I'll need much more than a peck to have you, won't I?"

"Was that a peck? I could have sworn it felt like a kiss on the cheek," I joked, seeing him narrow his eyes at me.

"Do you give kisses like that to your friends?" he growled.

"Sometimes." I shrugged, wanting to make him jealous.

"Zoey," he grunted like a caveman.

"I'm just kidding, governor." I gave him a gentle push on the shoulder, only to be surprised when he scooped me up into his lap, one arm around my back and the other around my legs.

"Don't mess with me, future Mrs. Fitzgerald..."

"I love to tease, governor," I mocked, holding firmly onto his shirt. "Now take me to my room. I need a bath."

He nodded, and I didn't even beg to be put down. I just allowed myself to live in the moment.

CHAPTER FORTY-FOUR

Zoey

It was my first day in William's house. At least he didn't insist that I sleep with him, which was a huge relief since it would have been hard to deny his request.

I sat on the bed, wearing one of my purple pajamas—shorts and a tank top—and ran my hand through my hair, tying it up.

I let out a long sigh as I looked around the room.

The day before, as soon as we arrived at the governor's house, my mother showed up with my suitcase full of clothes and my painting supplies.

William said he would have one of the rooms set up as my studio where I could work freely. Of course, I said it wasn't necessary, but clearly, I wasn't heard; he insisted that I needed a space that was entirely my own.

Before leaving, my mother made sure to organize the closet in the room where I would be sleeping, and I took the opportunity to chat with her and help her.

I THOUGHT WILLIAM WOULD be home, but all I got from him was a note with a red rose, saying he would be out all day to take care of some matters at the capitol and that a woman would come to see me—the housekeeper his mother had recommended.

Mrs. Dinner was pleasant and seemed to know everything about running a household, which was a relief. It meant I would have help, and together we chose a team that would be at my disposal for all necessary meals.

To me, all this was no big deal, considering my mother also had a housekeeper and a team managed by that housekeeper.

What was strange was that all of this was mine, or at least what William wanted. And surprisingly, I liked it—I enjoyed choosing the staff and working with Mrs. Dinner to keep everything organized.

WITH MY EYES TIRED, I decided to leave my painting room. When William said he would set up a painting room for me, I didn't think it would be done so quickly.

I went down the stairs and, since there wouldn't be any staff in the house today, I took the opportunity to rummage through all the drawers and cabinets in the kitchen, satisfying my curiosity and getting to know everything there.

All the cupboards were stocked, so I took out my phone and looked up a chocolate cake recipe.

I set all the ingredients on the counter. I searched for the mixer, found it, and placed it next to the food.

I knew the entire house was equipped with a *bluetooth* sound system, so I connected my phone to it and started playing my favorite artist, Taylor Swift.

The upbeat song echoed throughout the space as I prepared everything I needed, cracking the eggs into the bowl.

As I made the cake, dancing along with the music, I forgot about everything, including the fact that this house belonged to the governor and that he wanted it to be mine as well, which seemed crazy. The old Zoey would have accepted without a second thought, but this Zoey was hardened and afraid of being rejected a third time, prioritizing her own feelings.

Preparing the first part of the cake was easy. I took one of the pans, having memorized its location. I greased it and poured the chocolate batter in.

I put it in the oven, watching through the glass, and with a bit of batter on my hand, I brought my finger to my mouth, licking it.

"For a moment, I thought I was in the wrong house." I widened my eyes, turning my face and seeing the governor there.

"How... how did I not see you?" I asked, lowering my finger from my mouth.

"You were too focused on your task." He winked, taking my hand that was over my mouth. "I was envious of that finger."

"Governor." I gasped, pulling my hand away.

"I didn't know you had culinary skills." He gave a mischievous smile.

"Making a chocolate cake doesn't require much skill," I said, turning back to the center of my mess.

"I think I like this." I looked over my shoulder at him, not understanding what he meant.

"Like what?"

"This house being used, seeing you like this, with flour even in your hair." I immediately touched my hair. "Don't worry, you still look beautiful."

"You're strange," I said, making a face.

"And I thought you liked strawberries." The governor remembered our conversation.

"I do, but I only had ingredients for chocolate cake." I shrugged nonchalantly.

I started to clean up my mess while William stayed in the same spot. I noticed that he wanted to say something.

"Go on, governor, I know you want to say something." I crossed my arms, looking directly at him.

"You know me so well," he mocked, with a small smile.

"Well, it's not like I had an intense fixation on you for years." He raised an eyebrow, and I widened my eyes, realizing I had let something slip.

"What did you say?" William set his briefcase on a stool and walked around the counter towards me.

"Nothing." I bit my lip, knowing he wouldn't let it go.

"Don't play that with me; I heard what you said." I took a few steps back to the other side of the counter.

"It's nothing, William."

"Fixation, Zoey, did you have an intense fixation on me?" He kept walking towards me, while I circled around the island in the middle of the kitchen.

"Okay... okay..." I couldn't hide it. "I kind of knew everything about you; I loved watching you."

"Like a *stalker*?"

"I'm not a *stalker*." I grabbed a cloth from the counter, rolled it up, and threw it at the governor.

"From what you said, it sounds like you are." He laughed, catching the cloth I threw.

"I was just a good observer..."

"That's quite different from an intense fixation," he continued to mock.

"That was in the past! All of it was in the past." I wrinkled my nose in a self-assured manner.

"A past of what, less than two months ago? No one forgets someone that quickly." William stopped walking, as did I.

"But remember what was said to you," I said, upset.

"It just makes me feel even worse, knowing you were watching me, thinking of me as a man I clearly am not, for having hurt you." He exhaled heavily.

"Can we change the subject?" I bit my lip. "I don't want to talk about being almost a *stalker*..."

William suddenly burst out laughing, and I couldn't help but laugh along with him.

"So you're admitting it?" he asked, as if teasing.

"Come on, William, just say it already," I grumbled, rolling my eyes without revealing the truth.

"Alright, my most beautiful *stalker*. I have an event to attend today; your brother Malcolm will be there too. It's more of a political affair, and I'd like to take my fiancée with me. Will you accept?"

I wasn't prepared for that invitation.

"Fiancée? What fiancée doesn't even have a ring?"

As soon as I made that comment, the governor's eyes lit up, and he was clearly prepared for it.

CHAPTER FORTY-FIVE

William

At Zoey's words, my smile widened; it was exactly this topic I wanted to address regarding our engagement.

"Why are you smiling like that?" The way she asked was funny, as if she already anticipated what I was going to do.

I walked toward Zoey, and this time, she didn't walk away. She stood still, looking at me intently.

I put my hand in my pocket and felt the small velvet box containing the ring Scarlett had helped me with, using her friend's size.

"Our marriage proposal shouldn't be like this; it shouldn't be something forced. It has to be something just for us, mine and yours. Even if there wasn't this little thing inside you, I would still want you, want you with all my might. It's been hell being away from the woman who dominates my thoughts. This baby is like our new beginning. A sign that we need to be together. Know this, my little one, it will always be you. If you know me so well, you know I would never make this decision without being sure of what I wanted." Kneeling in front of her, I took the small velvet box from my pocket. "Will you marry me, Zoey Beaumont?"

She put both hands over her mouth, trying to suppress her astonishment.

"Is this... is this real?" she stammered with a choked voice.

"Yes, my little one, there has never been so much truth in my words as there is now," I declared, seeing her hands tremble.

We hadn't even decided how things would be or what the future would look like, but if there was one thing I had no doubts about, it was her. I wanted her by my side, wanted to come home more often and hear her music, knowing there was someone waiting for me every time I left the capitol.

"Yes, William, I accept," she finally said, making me calm.

It was only then that I realized I had been holding my breath. I held her small fingers and took the solitaire ring from the box, slipping it onto her finger.

I stood up, wrapping my arm around her waist, pulling her into an embrace, and lifted her so that her feet were off the ground.

Our eyes met again as I set her down.

"Is this a truce?" I asked, brushing my hand over her chin.

"Maybe." She bit the corner of her lip, taking a step back. "I want this wedding; don't think I don't, but a small part of me wants to feel more confident in you."

"Everything you've done for us just proves how perfect you are." I brought my lips to hers, giving a long, tender kiss because that was all Zoey allowed me to do.

Even though I wanted more, Zoey always remained reluctant, and all I wanted was her trust again.

I adjusted my tie in front of the mirror. It wasn't necessary to convince Zoey to come with me, as she loved these kinds of events and agreed almost immediately to accompany me.

She finished making her cake first, talking about her day, her conversation with the housekeeper, and the painting she had done. It was clear she enjoyed talking, and as a good listener, I loved hearing her.

When I stopped to think, it almost seemed like selfishness on my part not to have realized earlier that the woman who had all the qualities was right beside me and I had never noticed. Or maybe it was just my good friend side not wanting to cross a boundary with Malcolm, which eventually happened.

I never had a specific type of woman, but with Zoey, I came to realize that I did, the kind who loved to talk, had a sharp tongue, and a touch of good humor.

I turned away from my room; I could go downstairs, but my need to see the little woman led me straight to her room.

With two knocks on the door, I heard her approve my entry.

"May I come in?" I asked again, peeking my head into the room.

"Yes." She smiled, standing in front of the mirror.

Zoey looked incredibly beautiful in that burgundy dress. A slit on the side revealed her lovely leg, and she wore high sandals.

"Isn't it risky to walk in those high heels?" I asked concerned, approaching her.

"My belly doesn't even show, what risk could I run?" she questioned, confused.

"What if you trip?"

"That's never happened. It won't happen this time." I stood right behind her, seeing our reflections together in the mirror, where she held a black scarf in her hand.

I took the scarf from her hand, her little eyes fixed on me through the mirror.

"Do you trust me, little one?" I whispered, lifting the scarf and passing it over her eyes.

"William..." she gasped, unsure of what I was going to do.

"Better yet, don't answer my question now," I murmured close to her ear.

Zoey merely nodded. I picked up one of her fabrics from the counter, not knowing what it was.

"Put your wrists together," I requested, and she did.

From behind her, I tied her wrists. At that moment, I had Zoey entirely to myself.

"I could do whatever I wanted with you right now," I whispered very close to her ear. "And now, Zoey, do you trust me, trust me enough to know that I would never do anything to harm you?"

Her chest was rising and falling rapidly, clearly contemplating what I was saying.

"Yes, Will, I trust you," she said in a husky voice.

"That's exactly what I wanted to hear from your perfect little mouth." I ran my hand over her waist.

I wanted Zoey, desired that woman more than anything, but at that moment we weren't going to do anything, especially since I was late for the event and knowing her brother would be present, I didn't want to make a bad impression today.

Slowly, I lifted my hand, released her wrists, and then removed the blindfold, turning her to face me.

I brushed my hand along her cheek.

"You know, little one, I've always been sure that you never stopped trusting me." I smiled as I saw her roll her eyes.

"What you did was a trick," she declared, shamelessly moving her body closer to mine. "You know, Governor, you look very handsome in that suit."

I lowered my face and gently touched her lips.

"Baby, be careful with how you speak, unless you want your room invaded in the middle of the night..."

"Remind me not to leave the door locked." She winked, passing by me in a sensual manner.

With a soft laugh, I followed her.

CHAPTER FORTY-SIX

Zoey

As soon as the car stopped in front of the event, all the flashes turned in our direction.

"Great, they know it's us," William grumbled beside me.

The door was opened before I had a chance to say anything. First, the governor got out, and then I followed.

He extended his hand to me, and I took his large fingers while calmly placing my feet on the ground. With so many flashes in our direction, I didn't even know where to look. Luckily, William firmly held my waist, helping me walk since I had no idea where I was going, just keeping a smile on my lips.

We finally passed through an elegant golden-toned door, where a receptionist greeted us politely.

"Welcome, Governor Fitzgerald," she said, and he merely nodded.

We passed by her, his hand on my back the whole time.

"Have they told you that you were born to be in the spotlight?" he whispered close to my ear.

"Yes, Governor." I lifted my face, giving him a mischievous smile.

"You like to tease me, don't you?" He squinted his eyes.

"I like you without the swagger." I winked, clearly just trying to provoke him.

A waiter stopped in front of us, holding a tray with many glasses. William took one for himself, and I was about to grab one for me when he said:

"My dear?" he asked affectionately.

"Oh, I completely forgot." I shook my head. "Sorry..." My voice trailed off as I felt awful for forgetting about my baby.

"It's okay, it's all new," William said with a charming smile. "Is there water or some juice for my fiancée who can't have any alcohol?"

"Yes, sir, I'll get it right away." The waiter turned away.

"Thank you," I murmured with a small smile.

We both turned our gaze as footsteps approached us—it was Malcolm.

"Hi, brother." I gave him a big smile.

"How was it moving out of your mother's place to live with him?" He put his hand in his pants pocket. "If I didn't know him, I'd swear you did it on purpose."

Malcolm knew everything that had happened but apparently wanted to play with William, who maintained the dialogue with him.

"The good thing is that you know me, so there's no room for doubt." William never removed his hand from my back.

"Partially..."

"Please, don't start arguing," I interrupted my brother, since we were in public.

"I didn't come for a fight; it's more of a peace agreement." Malcolm extended his hand to William.

Initially, William did not accept, looking at the gesture with a frown as if he were considering whether it was genuine. Finally, he removed his hand from my back, switched his glass to the other hand, and shook my brother's hand.

"I would have done the same for my sister in that hospital. It's hard to accept that the man who went to college with me is now with my little sister. I know all your dirty secrets, and knowing that you're with my girl makes me a bit angry, but according to my grandfather, I need to get over it," Malcolm said.

"As for the dirty secrets, we can forget all that. I don't want her to have to worry about it; after all, it's the past." William curled his lip.

"And if you're not the best man for her, I'll have you castrated." My brother narrowed his eyes.

"I wouldn't doubt that." William gave a brief smile, the two of them released their hands, and the governor returned to holding me around the waist.

My brother asked several questions about me, wanting to know about my health and the baby. However, I didn't have much to say about the baby since I hadn't had a full consultation with the obstetrician yet. Due to all the events, we managed to reschedule the appointment for the next day so that William could accompany me without any issues.

Fortunately, we were interrupted by Zachary and Savannah, who had an even more prominent belly than the last time I saw her.

"Who would have thought?" The vice-president of America immediately teased his cousin.

"Don't start," William grumbled.

"I need to start because you were the one who said you'd never get married." Zachary made me smile.

"People who don't know you personally might swear you're serious men," I said, shifting the focus off William.

"*Shh*" Zachary made a gesture for silence, putting his hand to his lips. "No one can find out our secrets."

Savannah, who was standing next to him, rolled her eyes.

"What a big secret, husband," she said playfully.

"By the way, you look even more beautiful pregnant, Savannah," I said with a smile.

"I can't wait for this little one to be born." She let out a long sigh.

"Is she still traveling, Zach?" William asked, looking concerned.

"This is her last trip. She didn't even want to be here, but I have a stubborn wife who said she wanted to travel at least one last time." Zachary gave his wife a disapproving look.

"My obstetrician approved it, what's the problem?" Savannah made a face back at her husband. He bent down, holding her chin and kissing her forehead affectionately.

"My stubborn one." It was clear how much they loved each other.

Soon, the topic changed as more politicians approached, and when it came to family matters, they didn't discuss Fitzgerald's intimacies in front of others.

Gradually, I understood the purpose of the event. It was like a gathering with food and drinks, where various awards for citizens were decided, with nothing official, as there would still be private meetings.

William didn't let me leave his side for a minute, and what relieved me most was Malcolm's presence. The two even talked, unlike before the argument, and it seemed like they were slowly reconciling.

Zachary stayed with us the entire time, even practically forcing us to sit at one of the tables when his wife was feeling tired and wanted to sit down. This was wonderful for me, as I could sit next to Savannah and chat while the men talked politics.

CHAPTER FORTY-SEVEN

Zoey

When William wanted to leave, I almost sighed with relief. I had enjoyed the event, but I was even more excited about going home to rest.

During the entire car ride, we stayed silent, as he was busy with his phone, likely talking to his colleagues.

It wasn't long before we were parking in front of the governor's house. My door was opened right after his. We both exited together, and he quickly walked around the car to my side.

"Is everything okay?" he asked, perhaps noticing my silence.

"You were busy with your phone; I just didn't want to interrupt." I bit my lip, stating the obvious.

"You know you never interrupt," he said, but I didn't respond.

He unlocked the door and had already given me access, so I knew the code to enter and exit. I held onto the wall and took off my heels, leaving them on the floor.

I placed my bare feet on the ground as William hung up his jacket, and our eyes met.

"I don't know about you, but I'm dying to eat that chocolate cake," he said with a playful tone.

"I was practically drooling," I admitted.

We headed to the kitchen together. William quickly grabbed the plates while I took the utensils. The cake was in the center of the island where I had left it.

I sat on a counter as he took a seat across from me. It was the governor who sliced the cake, placing one piece on each plate, one in front of me and the other in front of him.

I didn't wait; I took a bite and closed my eyes at the taste as if I had never had cake before. A sigh escaped my lips.

"I guess I was craving chocolate cake."

"I can see that." I met his gaze, smiling.

"I must look like I haven't eaten in a year." I ran my tongue around my lips, wiping off the small crumbs.

"Actually, you look lovely." He winked, eating his first piece of cake while I watched, waiting for his reaction.

"So?" I couldn't help but ask.

"Divine, like the hands of the baker who made it." I let out a low laugh at his comment.

I ate another piece, then another, savoring each bite that made me sigh.

"I think I'm becoming addicted to you." I looked up, noticing that the governor was watching me as I ate.

"Trying to steal my stalker spot?" I teased, seeing a crumb of cake on my finger, bringing it to my mouth and eating it.

"Maybe being a stalker is a contagious disease and you passed yours on to me." He shrugged seriously, as if what he said was true.

"Heaven, we can't both become addicts." I smiled, biting the corner of my lip.

"Or we can, it just shows how well we match." He winked.

I didn't respond, going back to eating my piece of cake. Feeling full after finishing the last piece, I set my fork on the plate and looked at William.

"Zoey?" He called as he walked around the counter to stand beside me.

"Yes?" I whispered, feeling his long finger tuck my hair behind my ear.

"Will you sleep with me tonight?" He didn't look away, as if he was piercing through to the very depths of my soul with the intensity of his blue eyes.

"William." I gasped.

"I promise to do everything you expect from me..."

"And if I expect nothing?" I bit the corner of my lip playfully.

"I won't do anything, but I'm a Fitzgerald. We know how to be persistent." He winked again.

I placed my feet on the ground, stopping in front of him as he was blocking my way.

"What do you say, my little tornado?" he asked again, sliding his hand down my cheek.

"That I shouldn't regret this," a squeal escaped my mouth when he lifted me onto his lap. "William!" I scolded him, giving a light tap on his shoulder.

"You're so small that I love holding you in my arms." He laughed, heading towards the stairs.

I held onto his shoulder as if I were scared, though knowing he would hold me tightly no matter what. When we reached the top of the stairs, he turned towards his bedroom.

"I need to change; I need my pajamas." He turned his face towards mine.

"My shirts look perfect on you." I widened my eyes when he groped my backside.

"Governor, you're being very bold," I pretended to reprimand him.

Kicking the door open, it swung wide for us. He turned on the light, making me look around. It was exactly as it had been the last time we were here, when we had our second time together.

It was strange, considering back then there was no possibility of us being together, and now, I even had a ring on my finger and a marriage proposal from the man I had always dreamed of being with.

Stopping by the bed, he gently laid me down. His body covered mine, his face very close. I raised my hand and brushed it against his soft beard.

"Is it too strange for us to be here?" I whispered, biting the corner of my lip, anxious.

"No, or yes..." He smiled. "It's strange because it was always something forbidden to me. I never looked at you with interest, knowing you were my best friend's sister, and out of respect, I never looked at you; it was as if you were irrelevant. That was until that day in my car. You were anything but irrelevant; you were beautiful and sharp-tongued, going against everything I said, not to mention incredibly irritating with all that talk about marriage."

"But now you admit I was always right?" I said, running my hands along the back of his neck.

"Darling, you were always right about everything, about me, about us. It's as if you always knew, and I just needed to open my eyes to reality."

"I understand, Governor; you needed to rack your brains for a while before realizing that I was your ideal woman," I said, feeling a bit smug, doing what I did best—boasting.

"How could I have lived for so many years without your mischievous ways?" He lowered his lips to touch mine.

The tip of my tongue brushed his intentionally, wanting that kiss, and I felt William's large hand touch the side of my face.

"My little one," he murmured with our lips still touching. "I'm hopelessly in love with you, and I can't keep it to myself any longer; I can't hold it in anymore. I love you..."

Without waiting for him to finish speaking, I pulled his lip against mine, knowing it was what I had always wanted to hear. At that moment, the butterflies in my stomach were fluttering with happiness.

I needed my governor; I needed him completely, right there.

CHAPTER FORTY-EIGHT

William

I pressed my body against hers and demanded more and more from that kiss. I slid my tongue into her mouth, sucking it with a bit more force, and with my free hand, I squeezed her thigh, the one with the dress slit, feeling her skin under my fingers.

"William..." she sighed, scratching the back of my neck with her nail.

"Tell me, my little one, just don't tell me to stop," I said, trailing my lips down her neck, kissing her delicate, tingling skin.

"*Oh... don't stop, please, don't stop,*" she whined, trailing her fingers down the buttons of my shirt and opening the first one.

The V-neck of her dress made it easy to push the fabric aside and free one of her breasts, which I immediately began to suck with force, while nibbling and circling my tongue around her engorged nipple.

"Will..." I flashed a brief smile.

I got on my knees and began unbuttoning my shirt, tossing it on the floor. Zoey quickly grabbed the button of my pants. She opened it easily, making it clear she wanted me undressed. I stood up, removed my shoes and pants, and was completely naked.

I extended my hand, took hers, and stood her up in front of me. I unzipped the side of her dress, letting it fall to the floor. She was braless, only in panties, which I removed by sliding them down her legs.

Gently holding my chest, she pushed me so I sat on the bed. Zoey knelt in front of me and grasped my thigh. Her long hair cascaded over her shoulders. I held her chin and lowered my face as I felt my cock throbbing, begging for attention.

"My little one," I whispered with our lips touching.

"Yes, my governor." She bit the tip of my lip with a whimper. "Or should I identify myself as your slut..."

Hell, that woman had the power to test all my limits.

"Only if you're my exclusive slut." I bit her lip a bit harder, hearing her loud moan.

"Yours, only yours." She panted.

Aggressively, I intensified my tongue inside her mouth, giving her a rough, urgent kiss with our teeth clashing amid that luxurious act.

Zoey's hand moved up and covered the length of my cock, gripping it with precision and sliding down. Our kiss didn't stop at any moment as I splayed my hand through her hair and tilted her head back, releasing our lips.

"Now tell me, who is the only man who can dominate you?" I growled, looking at those red, swollen lips from all the biting.

"You, my governor." She seductively licked around her lips.

"*Fuck*! I'm addicted to you, insanely addicted," I grunted, lowering my hand to her waist, lifting her, and placing her on the bed with my body covering hers.

Unable to stop, I began placing thick kisses on her neck, moving down to her breasts, and when I reached the middle of her belly where our baby was growing, I caressed it, lowering my lips and leaving some kisses there.

"My..." I murmured, looking up at her. "I want this baby, I want you, I want the family we're going to build. I've never wanted something as intensely as I want this."

She touched my face with her finger.

"Please, never let me wake up from this dream." Her dark eyes, full lips, delicate features—everything about her made me fall even more in love.

"I promise." I slid my fingers between her legs and touched the center of her wet intimacy. "I promise to make you the happiest woman..."

"Do you really promise?" She rolled her eyes as I inserted a finger inside her.

"Yes, I promise with everything inside me." I brought my lips close to hers.

I began kissing her slowly while continuing to slide my fingers inside her, feeling her moisture.

"William," she moaned amid the kiss. "Take me as yours, fuck me, my governor, I beg you..."

"Anything my slut wants..." I pulled my fingers from her and put them in my mouth, sucking all her sweet nectar. "I can't waste something so delicious."

I spoke as I felt her legs wrap around my waist. I brushed the entrance of her little pussy with my cock, closing my eyes as I felt her walls squeezing me like soft cushions.

I placed my hand behind her neck, gripped her hair, and began thrusting with a bit more force. I always liked to fuck aggressively, but in this case, it was different; there was a baby inside her.

"My little one," I growled, our eyes locked on each other. "Let me know if I'm going too hard..."

"Oh... yes," was all she managed to say.

I couldn't stop; there was no way I could stay still amidst the pleasures of those delicious curves. I moved my lips to her mouth, kissing her with lust while continuing to fuck her.

All that could be heard in the room were our sighs, our sweaty bodies, and the love enveloping the entire atmosphere. Her nails traced my back, sure to leave many marks.

With her grip tightening, I knew she was reaching the peak of her pleasure, and that was everything I needed to give in with her. I gripped her hair more aggressively while my other hand clutched the bed sheets to avoid hurting Zoey. I moaned loudly, surrendered, and with one last thrust, I came inside her.

Avoiding putting all my weight on her, I simply embraced her body. She was so small, fitting perfectly in my arms.

Gently, I withdrew from Zoey, our eyes still fixed on each other. It was incredible how much I loved that woman; it felt like speaking my feelings out loud made everything easier, as if I had lifted a weight from inside me. I loved Zoey, and it was evident in every glance I gave her, in every moment we spent together, and in the many more we would have.

"Will," she whispered, tracing her finger over my chest as I lay down beside her.

"Yes, my little one?" I murmured lazily.

"Can we take a bath together like last time?" she asked with a sultry voice.

"No need to ask." I got up from the bed, and before she could expect it, I was already picking her up in my arms. "Everything for my future wife."

I winked seductively.

CHAPTER FORTY-NINE

Zoey

I felt a soft kiss on my cheek and slowly opened my eyes, spotting my governor there.

"Are you leaving me here alone?" I whispered through my sleepy voice.

"I need to work." He sat down beside the bed. He was fully dressed in his typical work suit.

"Will you be back late?" I pouted as I spoke.

"Today we have our baby's appointment; I wouldn't miss it for anything." He ran his hand over my smooth belly.

"Are you really sure you want to go?"

"Zoey, following your pregnancy is all I want. I want to savor every moment of our baby growing inside you, enjoy every curve that will form on your body." The way he spoke made his happiness clear.

I lifted my hand to touch the side of his beard, caressing his stubble.

"That's why I love you, you live everything so intensely," I said, not realizing that this was the first time I had said "I love you."

Last night, only he had spoken those words; I didn't want to force anything and ended up keeping my feelings to myself.

"Repeat it, please, repeat?" he asked, lowering his face.

"I love you, my governor," I said with a smile.

"Now, it's going to be even harder to go to work knowing I'm leaving my girl here, on my bed..."

"Governor, if your thoughts go any further, it will make everything harder," I teased.

"I need to go; I have to clear my schedule so all my personal belongings can be brought to this house today." He got up from the bed.

"So, it's official, this will be our home?" I asked excitedly.

"I thought it was already official. Are there still doubts?" William frowned in an amusing way. "If there are, get rid of them as soon as possible, because I won't let you leave my life anymore. It's mine now, and I will never let go."

"Governor, always so bossy." I sat on the bed, running my hand through my hair.

"Just taking care of what's mine." He winked playfully. "Before I forget, Mrs. Dinner is already here, along with some staff who are getting to know the house."

I nodded, watching him come towards me and give me another kiss on the lips.

"Call or text me if you need anything, okay?" he said, holding my chin.

"I think I'll spend the whole day so excited for the first appointment that I won't be able to think of anything else." A spontaneous smile brightened my lips.

After we returned from the hospital, the first thing William practically demanded was that I unlock my phone, almost having a meltdown when I said I wouldn't. That man was incredibly protective, but a kind of protective that cared for my well-being without depriving me of my personal life.

"I'm here to pick you up so we can go to our baby's appointment together."

"Our." I bit the corner of my lip at that realization.

"Mine and yours." He winked.

William turned towards the door, while I watched his proud stance. The man I had always dreamed of having by my side, whom I had briefly hated, hated for thinking we shouldn't be together, but who now, at that very moment, I loved even more intensely than the first time.

Was it possible to love the same person twice? Was it possible to love so intensely in such a short time? Whether it was or not, all I knew was that this man had my heart.

"My governor?" I called him as I always did in my dreams, but at that moment and from now on, it would always be real: me, him, and our future family. William turned, looking at me in confusion as to why I called him. "I love you, have a good day at work..."

I winked and blew a kiss into the air. William smiled to the side.

"My little one, I love you." He grasped the doorknob and left the room.

That would be just our first goodbye among all those that would come.

MY DAY WAS SPENT TALKING with Mrs. Dinner, getting everything officially organized for the staff who would be working here. I tried to paint a bit to get ahead on a painting I was working on for Mom's gallery.

My works were always used for landscape exhibitions, which was my main focus. I knew how to draw portraits of people, but what I truly loved were landscapes.

However, even painting didn't help distract me, as everything was centered around my first appointment. And now that it was over, it felt as though my heart could beat a sigh of relief.

William's hands held mine nervously, making it clear that he was also anxious.

We left the clinic together, but as soon as we stepped outside, a few men approached us wanting photos. William's security team positioned themselves in front and behind us, protecting us. The car door was opened so we could get in.

I thought William would get into the car, but what he did next surprised me. He held my waist, pulled me close, and I tilted my face up. Our eyes met.

"Damn it! I need to do this," he said quietly, hugging me, lifting me off the ground, spinning me around, and giving me a kiss on the lips, a delicate peck.

It was impossible not to smile at his craziness.

"I'm the impulsive crazy one here, did you forget?" I said, holding his face as I laughed.

"I want everyone to know, everyone to see how happy I am, how good you make me feel, and that I love you forever, my little big woman." Obviously, those photos would make a great headline, but at that moment, I didn't care about anything else, just him, my governor.

"I love you, my William."

"Yours and only yours..." We went back to sharing a long, lingering kiss.

Leaving that appointment and knowing everything was okay with our baby was a huge relief for both of us. We even managed to hear the baby's heartbeat, and the obstetrician had warned us that we might not be able to hear it, but in the end, we did.

Inside me grew our firstborn, strong and healthy. And now, nothing else mattered, just us.

If anyone had ever asked me if I really expected to end up engaged, and with a child of William Fitzgerald, I would have judged that person as crazier than me. But now I realized that perhaps there had always been a reason behind it all—the baby, our ending together, our story to be told as one, a couple.

He rejected me, but for our love, I gave him another chance, and my governor only proved capable of doing everything differently, the right way.

And that was why I was madly in love with him.

EPILOGUE ONE

Zoey

A Few Months Later...

The long dress swept across the beautiful hall, which had been completely decorated for our wedding. Everything was so incredible that I couldn't stop crying, but at least I had the excuse of pregnancy to blame it on.

Scar approached, looking stunning in a light pink dress, the color I had chosen for my bridesmaids.

"Who's the new Mrs. Fitzgerald?" she asked with that sly smile on her lips.

"A Fitzgerald." I raised my hand, showing off my delicate ring.

We hugged for the tenth time that night. I was happy, which made her happy too. Everyone was there—my family, William's family. Our wedding was the highlight of the year. Contrary to what everyone thought, William's supporters accepted me very well, even stopping me on the street for photos when I was alone.

Our baby was so anticipated that a fan club had already been created for him on social media, which might seem crazy, but as long as it didn't interfere with our personal lives, it was harmless.

"I didn't know Malcolm was dating," Scarlett said as soon as we pulled away from the hug.

"I confess I didn't know either." From a distance, I saw my brother with a blonde woman. "And she was hot."

"She really is..."

"Why the interest in my brother?" I asked, raising an eyebrow at her.

"Oh, nothing." Scar looked away from Malcolm.

"Scarlett?" I asked, crossing my arms.

"*Okay... okay...*" she leaned in and whispered in my ear. "Remember that day at Mr. Ralph's house?"

"Yes," I confirmed.

"Well, my brother and I... we... had sex..."

"What? And I never knew?" I widened my eyes.

"He made me promise not to tell anyone, not even you, since you had just found out about the pregnancy that same day, and I didn't, I kept it to myself. But it wasn't anything special, just sex." She shrugged, wanting to make it clear that it was nothing.

"Are you sure? It doesn't seem like that, my friend. I've shared all the disasters of my love life with you, so you can confide in me; it won't hurt." I smiled, holding her hand.

"Malcolm is experienced in bed, and you know how I am, all awkward. All the men I've been with were mediocre, just a quick affair, *goodbye and good luck*, and with him, it was different; it had everything, and for the first time, I had an orgasm. *But..., but...* I think he must have thought I was clueless, a sex novice, and he never spoke to me again, as if nothing had ever happened between us."

"So that's why you were acting strange with me?" She nodded, shaking her head.

"I'm so foolish to think he would care about someone as bland as me, with a nerdy look..."

"Scarlett, you're not any of that; you're a very attractive nerd. He's the one who missed out. I'll try to find out what happened, but please, don't tell anyone. We don't want the Beaumonts and the Fitzgeralds fighting again, especially now that they've started talking openly. — I patted her hands.

"Yes, I've kept it for so long, what's a little more? — She smiled to the side.

"I promise to let you know if I find out anything..."

"Find out what?" I felt my husband's large hand rest on my waist. I widened my eyes as I hadn't seen him there.

"*Oh*, it's about a dress that both of us want, and we made a bet, and since I won, she'll let me know when she finds it." Scarlett shrugged; she lied so well that even I almost fell for it.

My friend moved away, heading to her mother's side.

"What were you two talking about, *huh*?" I turned to face my husband.

"Girl talk, dear." I winked, touching his shoulder.

"I see, you two always with your little secrets." He squinted his eyes at me.

"Don't forget that Scar has always been my best friend, so there will always be little secrets. But nothing to worry about, as my heart belongs only to you."

William lowered his face, giving me a lingering kiss.

"Have I told you how beautiful you look tonight?" he murmured between kisses.

"Only about five times," I replied, running my hand along his neck.

"If it were up to me, there'd be at least six more..."

"Hey, it's time for the bride to throw the bouquet," my wedding planner called out.

"I'll be right back, my governor."

"I'll be waiting for you, my little one." We let go of each other's hands and I followed my wedding planner.

I climbed onto the stage where a band was playing, and as the music stopped, I approached the microphone to speak.

"The last time I caught a bouquet, it brought me luck, so the lucky one who catches this one will be fortunate." Everyone laughed at what I said. "I always said you'd be my governor, only you didn't believe it."

I spoke directly to my husband, who raised his glass and laughed.

I handed the microphone back, held my bouquet with both hands, counted to three in unison, and threw it, turning around immediately to see who caught it.

I burst out laughing when I saw that Hazel, who had become my best friend and was also Savannah's sister, had caught it. I reached out to grab the microphone again.

"I hope you already have someone in mind for our next wedding," I teased, knowing she didn't have anyone.

"If I had the certainty you have, I'd definitely run away from that guy," she joked. "I'll keep the bouquet, maybe the matchmaking saint will gift me a husband."

Everyone laughed, and soon the music started up again.

I walked down the side of the stairs where my husband was waiting for me, took his hand, and our fingers intertwined.

That day was the most magical of my life—my wedding, my husband, and inside me, our little Nathan.

William placed his other hand on my belly, caressing our son. There was no doubt he would be a great father, always attentive to me, wanting to know everything I needed, and even when he was at work, he would send messages. William was the typical doting dad, just as I always imagined he'd be.

Spending those months with him only made me more certain of what I always wanted—to be by his side. The man I chose to be mine.

EPILOGUE TWO

William

Four years later...

I pulled back the curtain in my office and spotted my little whirlwind running around on the lawn. Nathan was chasing after his *baseball* that he had received from his grandfather, my father.

I was never as spoiled by them as my children were. When they said that grandparents spoiled their grandchildren, this is what they were talking about.

My mother couldn't see my daughter dawdling without immediately asking if she needed anything. Even at two years old, Mia had already realized she could do whatever she wanted when the grandparents were around.

A knock on my door made me turn my face. There was no need to ask her to come in, as she was already walking through the door.

"Hello, my little one." I moved towards her.

"I woke up alone in bed today." Zoey made a small pout with her lip.

"I needed to make some calls." I placed my hand on her waist, pulling her close.

"Are you working from home today?" she asked excitedly.

"Yes." I brought my lips close to hers.

Unlike my cousins who always demanded high-profile political positions, all I wanted was to stay in California with my family, my parents, my wife, and my children. That was enough, it was paradise.

"You haven't forgotten that today is Mia's ballet class, have you?" Zoey bit her lip.

"Nothing will make her give that up, will it?" I made a face.

"Over time, I know she'll want to quit."

Mia was a determined little girl. She constantly complained about not liking ballet, but she kept going. The worst part was that my daughter had no talent for dancing whatsoever.

Neither I nor Zoey wanted to take her out of it unless she wanted to quit. We were just waiting for her to make the first move.

"I'll go with Mia to her ballet class then," I said awkwardly.

"If you want, I can go." Zoey forced a smile.

"You take Nathan to baseball, and I'll stay with our little genius." I ran my hand along her cheek.

"What did we do to end up with two such clever kids?" Zoey teased affectionately.

"I guess that's what you get when you combine the genes of two stubborn people," I said, running my hand along her waist. "Shall we have breakfast?"

I always waited for her to wake up so we could have breakfast together. Sometimes, when Zoey stayed up late painting in her studio, she would end up sleeping a bit longer in the morning.

"Let's go, because our little whirlwind is already back there driving his poor babysitter crazy." Zoey sighed at what I said.

"That boy must wake up before the sun rises," she whispered.

"This one's going to be a handful," I joked.

"Has Mia already woken up?"

"As a proper princess, she's still catching up on her beauty sleep," I said the words that Nathan always repeated about his sister.

Knowing that Mia would wake up soon, we headed to the breakfast table.

That was our somewhat chaotic routine, but it always worked out in the end. When we had Nathan, it was like adding a new member to the house, a little baby whose cries I loved echoing through the walls. Watching my firstborn grow was the most perfect thing.

As Nathan grew and reached his first birthday, Zoey said she wanted another child, another member for that big house. Of course, her request felt like winning the lottery to me. I had always wanted to be a father of two, and when we found out we were having a girl, it was like completing our puzzle. Our two children, so clever, smart, and joyful, our kids, our little mixtures.

If I could do everything differently, I certainly wouldn't, because it would mean not having Zoey by my side.

My little whirlwind, who showed me that life could be lighter and more beautiful to live, changing all my convictions and making me fall hopelessly in love with her.

Not a day went by that I didn't feel incredibly lucky to have those perfect people by my side.

THE END.

Did you love *Whirlwind of Desire*? Then you should read *When Tornadoes Collide* by Amara Holt!

When Tornadoes Collide is a gripping, emotionally charged romance that sweeps you into the high-stakes world of **politics** and **passion**. Christopher, the youngest president in U.S. history, is a man driven by **control** and **power**. After losing his wife in a tragic accident, he closes himself off from life's pleasures, focusing only on his political career.

Enter Hazel, a bold, **free-spirited** law student and intern at the family company. With her sharp wit and boundless energy, Hazel is everything Christopher is not—**wild**, **carefree**, and unafraid to challenge the rules. When their worlds collide, sparks fly, and the White House becomes the stage for an intense **clash of wills** and undeniable **attraction**.

As Christopher's carefully constructed life starts to **unravel**, Hazel forces him to confront the man he's become. But can their passion survive the pressure of **power**, grief, and the public eye?

When Tornadoes Collide is a story of **love**, **loss**, and the electrifying power of two forces destined to meet. If you're looking for a romance filled with **fiery chemistry**, unexpected twists, and emotional depth, this book will sweep you off your feet.

About the Author

Amara Holt is a storyteller whose novels immerse readers in a whirlwind of suspense, action, romance and adventure. With a keen eye for detail and a talent for crafting intricate plots, Amara captivates her audience with every twist and turn. Her compelling characters and atmospheric settings transport readers to thrilling worlds where danger lurks around every corner.